DREAMLESS UTOPIA

OMDRA SIX

Thanks to my friend Jeremiah of Lakeland who helped when it was needed and who also inspired the Deven character.

1

The copters buzzed through the sky like monstrous
bumble bees swarming toward the city. Panicking catwalk
strollers broke into flight. They elbowed and shoved
one another, rebounding off the restraining fence, clawing for
the safety of the enclosed city whose shiny interior gleamed in
the distance. Some people didn't run. The
mindless merely shuffled onward like zombies, heads

bowed and arms dangling, while others watched the lowering aircraft over their shoulders, not caring.

Deven and his friend Sten cupped their hands over their noses and mouths as they knocked the mindless and the casual strollers aside. The buzzing of the copters and the hiss of their deadly ammonia spray grew louder and louder. A curtain of moisture fell like fine rain and was blown over the catwalk by the wind, spurring the runners on.

The herd stampeded to the end of the catwalk and crushed into the city through the narrow entrance, Deven and Sten spinning out of the midst of the chaos. Their nostrils were saved. But the sweet air had been bleached and Nature was once again subdued.

"Whew! I wish they'd warn us when those damn things start on their atmosphere cleansing rounds," complained Deven, a well-developed man of thirty-seven. He had a triangular shaped face, intense brown eyes, and was of a darker complexion which was very distinct in this society of genetically engineered people.

"What a refreshing smell!" said Sten, a lean, long-legged man who always seemed to be staring at something in the distance."It's hard to believe that some don't like it."

"The plague was in 2163. You'd think the bugs were all dead by now."

"No, 2164. You don't want to risk another outbreak, do you?" Sten sucked in some of the city's cool, metallic air.

"Another outbreak! You must be dreaming. That disinfectant can kill any bug."

Breaking away from the pack that had escaped the antisepticizers, they merged with the crowd on the concourse. Ixxendra was built in the standard shopping center design and had four mezzanines connected by escalators.

"I once flew in one of those air-cleansing copters," Deven said. "It was when we were doing an aerial survey of the site. I even piloted the thing for awhile."

Deven was head of a 134 member crew that'd been excavating the ruins of a mid-21st century city for the past five years, a government sponsored project whose purpose was to uncover a secret vault believed to have been constructed beneath the city.

Deven shook his head as if at a joke.

"They take the trouble of surveying the site, training over a hundred people in the science of archaeology, supplying heavy machinery and even extend the monotrain rail all the way to the excavations and we'll probably dig up nothing but a lousy old vault filled with pornographic magazines."

"What makes you say that?"
"Because the corporalites are as loony as everybody else. They probably made their plans for the dig on a bet a couple of them made."

"You don•t really believe that?"

"As devoutly as I believe in Santa Claus."

"I didn't think you did."

"I don't!" Deven snapped. "What a nutty religion this society dreams up -- based on a legendary figure who only children used to believe in. But I guess it's not any more stupid than the government's policy of population control. They try to make us believe that miniscule babies are contained in sperm cells yet they sterilize women for birth control. And it's nothing less than insane to use deathmen to bump off perfectly healthy citizens in the name of population adjustment."

"We're not all perfect."

"I'll say. And who can we blame for this ludicrous condition of society — the government.

Don't the corporalites try to keep everybody confused, especially with that News Bureau where they mix phony stories with real ones so we're always kept guessing?"

Sten, who produced fictitious stories for the News Bureau, cleared his throat.

"Sorry. Wasn't meaning to insult you."

"Good, because the reason I wanted to talk to you was to ask about doing a story from your site."

"Not considering a factual documentary, are you?"

"Who'd know the difference?"

Deven nodded.

"I've already got the story plotted out," the newsman said, his gaze cast into the distance of lustrous walls and crisscrossing escalators. "I'm going to show your astounding discovery of a horde of mutant humans who've been living in an underground vault since the destruction of the city. You'll have to destroy them in the end, naturally."

"Naturally." Deven pursed his lips, lips sharply etched by years of free thinking. "And where the South Pole am I supposed to get these mutants?" These days, the South Pole was synonymous with Hell, the North Pole with Heaven.

"I'll supply all you need. I have a large crew of

actors at my disposal."

"I assume you've already got clearance from the city council, so why are you bothering to ask me?"

"Because we're friends. I owe you the courtesy."

When children, they'd gone through the maturation process together at the state run programming center and had formed as close a relationship as could be in this emotion blunted society. They used to play a game together against the data disseminating computer. The object was to block the electrical impulses shot directly into the brain, and whoever did so the longest, which was usually Deven, was the winner. Deven preferred blocking social conditioning impulses, while Sten fought off mathematics.

"When do you plan to begin your story?"

"Soon as possible."

"Oh, well, guess that means we'll have to hide the

weapons we're making for our revolt and burn the top secret plans," Deven joked.

"Don't say such a thing even in jest."

The tall newsman reeled in his gaze and peeked over his shoulder at a mechanical dustpan that crawled up behind him, snapping its jaws in a demand for refuse. Sten screwed his hands into his pockets.

"Still feeding those damn things, huh?" Deven said.

"You know how annoying they are if you don't."

"They're annoying either way."

Sten tossed a piece of crumpled paper to the glossy floor and the dustpan-eavesdropping device gobbled it up as eagerly as it did conversations.

"Not even a thank you." Deven grunted.

"You spend too much time away from the city," Sten observed. "You're losing contact with civilization. I still don't know how you can bear it out there in that ...that Claus forsaken wilderness."

"I've gotten used to it. It's not so bad."

How could Deven tell him about the fresh, pine-scented springtime air, or about the mystical silence before a summer storm, or how delicious apples tasted when warmed by the sun, or how satisfying a heated shelter was after escaping the freezing rage of a blizzard? Sten wouldn't understand; and Deven's admission of his true feelings would only help mark him as an oddity or worse.

"Why do you want to do a story from my site all of a sudden?" the archaeologist asked.

"A fresh, imaginative story like this one might move me one step closer to being promoted to head of the

News Bureau, then maybe even farther up."

"You're not dreaming, are you?"

"I don't believe so."

Deven abruptly cut to the left. He walked toward a building that was fitted with a row of port hole like windows and peeked inside. "Have a gander in here," he said, "and see the kids with their brains plugged into the master computer." This was an educational programming center.

Sten tried not to listen, declining to look inside.

"Know how kids used to learn?" Deven asked, pushing away from the wall. "They used their home computers, the computers didn't use them. That's just one of the bits of history I learned at the site."

Sten gravely shook his head. "Idea formation like that can lead to a thought transfusion."

"Rayniss keeps me in line."

"Rayniss?"

"My latest roommate. We've been living together for about six weeks now. She's a real believer in doctrine — 'dream less and live longer' and all that rot."

"She sounds very well adjusted. I suggest that

you continue the relationship."

"I hope to."

Roommates rarely stayed together longer than six months, though there wasn't any illegality in doing so.

A patrol robot swept down the concourse, furrowing the crowd ahead.

"Idiots!" spat Deven. "Treating that overgrown garbage can like a god, trampling one another to get out of its way. I used to program patrol robots before being assigned to the site, and they're pretty stupid without proper instructions."

Deven took a long step to the right to block the path of the mighty, seven foot tall machine with the sledgehammer head, but was yanked back by Sten.

"That was foolish!" barked the newsman. "You could've been reported for obstructing the route of a law enforcement device."

"If we had patrol robots at the site they'd get out of our way, not vice versa."

"They'd have too. You'd all be corpses, lying dead in their paths for obstructing them."

The two men stepped over to a nearby xeleporter. These were devices that looked like telephone booths and which provided instantaneous transportation on voice command. Every public and private place in the city had at least one xeleporter, and they were dispersed throughout the concourses.

"You sure you want to do this story?" Deven asked.

"Of course."

"Be at the commuter station tomorrow at nine. I'll give you a personal tour of the site, or would you rather shoot the whole thing on a stage?"

"No, I want complete authenticity, even if it means enduring a whole day out there."

"Maybe you'll like it." Deven entered the xeleporter. He was putting aside his principles to help his friend.

"I doubt I'll like reverting to a caveman."

Shrugging, Deven issued destination instructions, then vanished.

2

Deven materialized in his apartment, stepped out of the xeleporter, and was attacked by his roommate, naked and lust driven.

"Give me a baby!" Rayniss cried. She'd always wanted to be a whore. Whores were inmates of breeding centers.

"Please give me a baby!" Rayniss moaned, hugging and kissing the archaeologist. "Hurry!"

"I ... I'll do the best I can," he said, struggling with her toward the bed on the raised level.

Deven fought from his clothes, then performed the body sensitizing ritual with the young woman. Hands oozing with gobs of tingling lotion, they spread it over each other's flesh, then massaged it in with body friction, rubbing chest against chest, stomach against stomach, thigh against thigh, knees, calves, buttocks, then backs. It was tribal. It was bliss.

Bodies ripe for lovemaking, burning and quivering, they dropped onto the old-fashioned brass posted bed, twisting in a hold of passion, crying out with delight. Rolling each other in rapture, they smeared syrupy kisses on each other's lips, their lubricated bodies making delicious slushing sounds.

"Give me a baby!" Rayniss commanded.   "Hurry!"

Deven deflated atop her, spent, and shared the rippling tremors of her body as she quieted. Then the two lay flaccid, glued together by each other's sweat and the sensitizing lotion whose jasmine fragrance mixed with the odor of perspiration into a sensuous scent.

Rayniss demanded this type of lovemaking, the only kind that could satisfy her and she always had to be satisfied.

insert dream

"Did it work?" the woman sighed, stroking her greasy stomach. "Am I pregnant now?"

Deven gave an indefinite, "Who knows?" No other roommate had made him feel as satisfied after sex as Rayniss because with her it was more than just a physical experience — for him.

He gazed through the haze of contentment at the cooing woman. She was still now, her narrow eyes closed, her boyish, sandy hair ruffled, and her sleek body glistening. Rayniss was a mirage. Deven longed for her affection, her emotional warmth, but they were things she didn't possess, qualities drained from her as they'd been drained from nearly everyone else by a brutally emotionless society. Was there a chance he could put them back into her?

After a brief rest, Rayniss and Deven arose and stepped over to the kellator in the corner, a device that looked like a shower enclosure but used heat waves rather than water to cleanse dirt, bacteria, and other impurities from the skin. Swirling pink mist swept over them with a breezy touch and steamed their skin with violet-scented purifiers.

Deciding to spend the evening playing video games at one of the amusement centers, Rayniss dressed in a knee-length, see-through gown that was swept with blue strips of aluminum that hung from a close-fitting collar, and Deven pulled into a casual one piece jumpsuit.

A short step down and they were in the living area. Antiques that Deven had appropriated from the site clashed with the glossy gray walls and floor and with the wide news screen on the wall. A pair of old-fashioned well-stuffed easy chairs faced the news screen with contempt, a landscape oil painting of Wisconsin woodland fought with the wall, a 22nd century lamp with a porcelain base that bloomed in a floral design sat defiantly on the roll-top desk in the wall niche, and a kaleidoscopic Persian rug lay as a challenge before the xeleporter. Only the four foot tall pleasure pole in the middle of the room couldn't be camouflaged, though Deven sometimes used it as a hatrack.

The matronly looking broadcaster on the news screen announced, "Rumors still persist that some of the old cities are currently inhabited by bands of lunatics who've fled there from the safe areas. Despite the cleansing of most suburban locations and small towns by controlled nuclear detonations, large portions of many former major population centers such as Chicago, New York, Los Angeles, and New Orleans are still intact and supposedly providing places of refuge for the insane."

"Too bad we never found a cure for the plague that wiped out most of the planet's population," Deven off-handedly remarked as he plucked a food wafer from the wall dispenser and fell into one of the easy chairs. "Of course, that'd be pretty hard since we never found its cause, either."

The broadcaster continued, "Plans to dispatch specially equipped military units into these areas to forcibly remove the misguided inhabitants have been proposed by many city councils, but none has yet been approved due to the high cost and lack of useful return to be gained from the undertaking."

"I wonder if the report is true." Deven munched the tasteless wafer. "The lucky devils who escaped — supposedly that is."

"Lucky?" Rayniss also snatched a wafer from the dispenser. "Who in his right mind would want to leave the safety of a civilized city to live in infected rubble?"

The petite woman crossed the room with a skip in her step and sat beside Deven. Even her walk enticed him, a walk that was different from the calculated, lifeless styles of other women, having an ease and fluency that portrayed an independent personality and a subtle conceit. Her erotic body movements while twisting in front of one of the video games was what had first attracted Deven to her.

"What about the cat?" Rayniss asked, calling the simulation feline of flexible neo-plastic and synthetic fur.

"What about it?"

"Look how it's acting." The malfunctioning device leapt into the woman's lap in slow motion. "It's got to be fixed."

"Yeah, I'll take it in to the shop. I'd rather have a real cat, though."

Live cats weren't permitted in the city so mechanical ones were purchased, as well as mechanical mice, hamsters, dogs, birds, guinea pigs, and even gold fish.

"Would you prefer real mice, too?"

"Claus! This artificial stuff is so lousy."

"Deven, you've been at that archaeological site too long. You're even starting to talk different from the rest of us. Some of the strange words you use ."

Everyone was programmed to speak grammatically correct by the linguistic computer,though many eventually slipped in their usage of it.

"Sten told me I'd been out there too long, too." Deven finished his meal. "Okay, when I start preferring real mice I'll ask to be transferred to a city job."

It'll be too late by then."

"It ain't so bad." How could he confide to her that he enjoyed his time at the site and that he was content to commute back and forth from it to the city and take advantage of both environments? That'd only alienate her from him.

The matronly figure on the news screen was replaced by a fatherly one. "A special report just came into our local newsroom here in Ixxendra. The city of Tarro, Illinois has just filed a complaint against Ixxendra with the National Board of Justice citing thirty-two counts of copyright enfringement of local news stories. The city council of Tarro, a municipality located ten miles south of the border from us, warns of severe consequences if settlement is not quickly made in the form of energy allocation. We will keep you up to date on this fast breaking story as details come in. Now, back to network coverage of the latest volcanic eruption in Lecoya, Mexico."

"Copyright infringement!" Deven howled. "What a bunch of malarkey."

"A bunch of what?"

"Never mind."

Deven's vocabulary had been greatly colored and expanded by exposure to the mass of literature he'd discovered at the site, most of which he'd read before feeding it to the incinerators per orders.

"I've had enough news for awhile,"Rayniss said, finishing her wafer. "Let's go to the amusement center."

She and Deven went to the xeleporter, gave destination instructions, then disappeared. En route, they were kept in suspension — put on hold — for several minutes before materializing because of the backlog of passengers.

Afterwards, Deven suggested, "Let's walk next time."

"Oh, that's too old-fashioned."

Giddy and warmed from the wait, Rayniss skipped out of the xeleporter and into the vast, lustrous hall of chrome walls. The scene was frenetic as video game players twisted and bobbed and contorted before their machines in moves a gymnast would applaud. All just to keep their rocket ships from being annihilated, their knights from being devoured, their battleships from being sunk, and so on and so on.

Shiny reflections flashed about the new arrivals as they searched for a vacant machine. Finding one, Deven stabbed it to life with his account data card.

"I hope we win a lot of credits," Rayniss bubbled, her small, triangular face pressed eagerly up to the screen. "There's a new multi-wave navel nuzzler I've been dying to get." Instead of useless points, monetary units could be amassed, or lost.

The game began and Rayniss worked the controls with single-minded intensity, her eyes wide and her lush tongue playing over her lips. Keeping one hand on her flicking hip, Deven enjoyed the feel and the sight of her twitching young body, wishing he could have her for a permanent roommate.

"Forgetting is succeeding," a voice repeated in hypnotic monotone over the public address system. Each day the mind-lulling slogan was different, the result of long hours of research by government psychologists. Although their messages sounded harmless, and even absurd, their true purpose was neither.

"Stop that!" Rayniss barked at the man working the

machine alongside of hers.

Grinning, he banged her hip for the fifth time.

"Stop it! You're disturbing my play!"

"Yes, that's my intention."

Deven awoke from his mild trance.

"Will you stop it!" This time she shouted.

Deven stepped over to the culprit, telling him,
"Keep your mind on your own game, you jerk!"

"Maybe I prefer hers. Jerk? I didn't jerk. Very
colorful language - dark man."

The tall, handsome man with the arrogant smile
turned toward Deven, revealing the insignia of a
dagger over his heart which identified him as a deathman,
an executioner employed by the city to murder victims
chosen to die for population control.

"She'd rather play her game by herself," Deven
growled.

"Forgetting is succeeding."

"See this?" The deathman pointed to the dagger.
"I can have any woman I want." Deathmen were a
privileged class.

"Not this one." Deven snarled.

"We'll see about that."

"Yeah, let's."

Rayniss was gratified by all this attention paid her

and was faintly smiling.

A nearby patrol robot saw what was happening and sped to the scene.

"Present your identification cards," it ordered.

The men inserted their I.D.'s into a slot in the robot's chest. A few angry seconds passed.

"Forgetting is succeeding."

"Deven WY6, you are ordered to locate another video machine."

His card popped back out.

"Trall LR2, you may resume play but will be kept under guarded observation."

The deathman ripped his card from the robot, telling Deven, "Now, me and the young woman can get acquainted without your interference."

"Forgetting is succeeding."
Deven yanked his account data card from the video machine.

"Aw, and I was winning, too," whined Rayniss.

She could've inserted her own account card and resumed play at this machine, but a loyalty she didn't understand made her leave with Deven.

Deven returned home alone because Rayniss had a friend to visit. He had one of his typical altercations with the newsscreen which was also a mechanically operated observation device. Deven was tired and sat in a sofa to take a nap.

"Sleeping outside the slumber receptacle is not allowed," the voice from the screen warned him.

Deven responded by placing a handy mannequin inside of the slumber receptacle as usual. This time the security system noticed.

"Get off my back!" Deven shouted at the screen.

"I am a disembodied voice. It is impossible for me to be on your back."

"You're a lousy nuisance."

"You need my assistance."

"What I need is a nap."

"Then go to your slumber receptacle."

"I'm already in it. Can't your sensors tell you that?"

"Then how can I be talking to you now?"

"You must be talking to yourself," Deven said.

"But you are answering me."

"No, you must be hearing things. Having hallucinations."

"But I'm a disembodied voice."

"Maybe, but you're still having hallucinations. You should see a psychiatrist."

"But I see a physical entity sitting before the screen. You must be there."

"No, you're seeing things. That's bad."

"I...I must shut down and analyze this."

The screen turned off. Deven took his nap.

3

When closing one's eyes, a twilight blue formed under the lids like a mist. There weren't any dreams, any sensations, not even the sense of sleeping; there was nothingness, not even time.

The same thought that was in the mind when retiring in the slumber receptacle was there when rising.

A minute could've passed, or a year; the only way of knowing was by checking the calendar clock on the rim of the receptacle after waking; which was the first thing a person did. Everyone was a potential Rip Van Winkle. However, though a person might sleep twenty years he'd only age five because the aging process was considerably slowed while in the slumber receptacle, life expectancy now 157 years.

Dreams repressed during the slumber period sprang from the subconscious while awake as intense, micro-second hallucinations and disrupted reality. But the atrocities done to logic at these times were never perceived, though their affects were profound.

Unseen faces projected from walls, unheard voices shrieked in the silence, sudden scenes of torture and butchery were performed in full view of the subconscious.

And there were rapturous dreams, too; dreams of outrageous sexual abandon and feats of ecstatic delight. The pleasure of an orgy could be experienced within a micro-second of dreaming, but these types of dreams were rare. It was the monstrous and the grotesque that usually overwhelmed a person and left him straddling the precipice between reality and fantasy. And thus was society on a whole.

This night, Deven slept a short while on the sofa and dreamed of a real event he'd once had confessing a sin to Santa Claus, per common custom, sitting before the red-coated man who was in a rocking chair. Santa began by asking why Deven was there.

"Because I kicked a dustbot off a ledge."

"Why would you do that?"

"It pissed me off."

"Pissed you off, my son?" said Santa. "What does that mean?"

"Made me angry. So I kicked the bastard, you bloated billiken."

"Should you have kicked that bastard?"

"No, I should have picked it up and busted it to pieces."

"Are you sorry, then, for what you did?"

"Yeah, I guess in that way - sure."

"Have you done any nice deeds I should know about? So I don't mark you down as only naughty."

"Yes, I added some words to the vocabulary of a security robot that stopped me yesterday."

"And what were those words?

"Shit fuck and then, fuck shit."

"Good, I'll write those down in my book, too."

"Are we done here, goofy?" Deven asked Santa.

"Your penance. I instruct you to throw a handful of refuse to the next dustbot you come upon."

"How about a stick of dynamite?"

"Fine, my son. Do that, and cause no more trouble."

dream

"See you later, pal. And keep those damned elves off my back, will you?"

Deven got up and left.

Then he awoke and joined Rayniss in the slumber receptacle.

4

    The green light blinked on, and the lid opened. A pleasing warmth like sunshine touched their naked bodies, restoring life and nourishing them with the glow of radiant energy. From toes to the top of the head the reviving warmth gradually spread, taking five minutes to resuscitate the occupants of the slumber receptacle; and their eyes opened like morning glories.

"Is it tomorrow?" Rayniss concernedly asked, her mouth flavored with honey.

Deven checked the calendar clock and winked. "It's okay, we haven't overslept."

Sitting up, Rayniss stretched, pulling taut her onion round breasts. She glanced at the news screen in the living area and suddenly deflated. "Oh, no! Look!" she moaned, pointing.

A message from the surveillance center had been electronically typed on the bottom of the news screen, reading —

> DEVEN WY6 — REPORT TO BREEDING
> CENTER ON THE 23rd DAY OF THIS
> MONTH AT THE HOUR OF 16. SEXUAL
> ACTIVITY PROHIBITED TILL THEN.

The twenty-third was three days away, three whole days of abstinence, or so Rayniss thought.

"So what?" Deven shrugged. "I'll gladly go to the breeding center, but I'll be damned if I'm giving up sex in the meantime."

"You mean we'll still ..."

"Sure. I never obey the orders of imbeciles."

"I've never known anyone who went against the prohibition of sex."

"Now you do."

They climbed out of the receptacle and fell onto the bed, rolling in embrace, all the more aroused because lovemaking was now illegal for them.

"I was proud of you last night," Rayniss confided between kisses.

"Why?"

"Because of how you faced that deathman over me."

"Ah, deathmen are just a bunch of cowards. It doesn't take any courage to kill an unsuspecting victim while he's sleeping in a slumber receptacle."

"Still, what you did felt good. I can't really explain the feeling, but it was good."

"Yeah, and this will be, too."

The sexual romp began in earnest, and this time they both felt the emotional impact.

Afterward, they hurried into the living area — it was 8:51 — plucked a couple of wafers from the dispenser, and munched them before the news screen.

A bright-faced, young female newscaster was excitedly reporting, "Late last night the city of Tarro, Illinois recalled its ambassador from Ixxendra. When word of this reached president Drape in the nation's capital at Delltex, Iowa, he promptly dispatched a team of negotiators to each city. Other than taking this action, however, he is powerless to prevent war between the two sides. Meanwhile, the National Board of Justice is still considering Tarro's request that sanctions be levied against Ixxendra but is not expected to reach a decision before the week's end."

"Do you think it'll mean war?" Rayniss asked.

"Who even knows if the story's real or not?"

It was 8:57. Rayniss and Deven rushed to the xeleporter, she to go to her job as inventory monitor over retail outlets, and he to go to the commuter station to meet Sten.

The commuter station was a long lobby of mostly empty space. Trips by monotrain would be taken from here to outlying scientific and technological plants which were too distant to be reached by xeleporter.

Multiple-armed mechanical maintenance devices, cousins to the refuse gobbling dustpans and just as proficient at eavesdropping, vigorously polished the shiny silver walls, springing up and down on long spindly legs like robot spider monkeys. Archaeologists in orange uniforms milled about the lobby and other commuters waited on the steel benches.

Deven was met by his chief assistant, Brogg. He

was of stocky build, had curly black hair that looked like
steel wool, and squinting eyes that made him seem like
he was always looking for something. Deven thought
he and Sten complimented each other, one looking near,
the other far.

Moments later, Sten arrived, striding from the row
of xeleporters, seemingly gazing past Deven and Brogg.
Introductions were made and they then got in line to
pass through the sensor screen prior to boarding the
train. Aside from the outdoor catwalks, which were
ten stories above ground level, this was the only exit
from the city and a person needed a special pass to get
through the electronic screen or be paralysed on contact
with it. The city council claimed that this was a
precaution to keep outsiders from sneaking in.

The trip began. The monotrain, a sleek, long vehicle,
surged through a short stretch of meadow on a single
ground rail and then plunged into a dense forest dominated
by oak, maple, and pine trees.

"See, it's not so bad out here," Deven assured Sten.

The newsman sat rigidly in his seat as if at a
horror movie and flinched from the tree branches whipping
by the windows.

"Something wrong?" Brogg chided. "Those are only

trees. They won't hurt you."

The shock of being assigned to the archaeological site five years before had almost driven Brogg mad, and to compensate he developed an abnormal hatred of society and love of Nature. Deven was required to report his condition, but hadn't. He disliked regulations, despised government meddling, and wouldn't be an informer.

"What can you tell me about the reports about people going back to the old cities?" Deven asked the newsman.

"You mean the escaped lunatics?"

"Then it's true? People can safely return?"

"True? I can't say. You know how the news is made."

"Yeah, and I know that some of the stories are true. Is this one?"

"I really can't answer that."

"Why not?"

A nightmare interrupted Sten's thoughts and his face paled.

"Sten, why can't you tell me about those reports?"

"Uh, can't give away trade secrets." He slowly recovered from the bad dream.

"What about Tarro pulling out its ambassador?" Brogg questioned, his eyes scrunched even tighter.

"That a trade secret, too?"

"It's difficult to say."

"What's so difficult about a straight answer?"

"Because I don't know the truth."

Deven patted the newsman on the knee and laughed. "Don't feel bad, I doubt if anybody around here knows the truth about anything ."

The three men sat back for the rest of the five mile journey. Soon the monotrain skimmed to a halt beside a fifty-yard-long, one story aluminum building that was the archaeological site's headquarters. It housed laboratories, medical facilities, storage areas, and living quarters -- a small city in itself.

Deven led the passengers onto the receiving platform. The fresh spring air scented with budding vegetation nauseated Sten, but he endured it. However, it was too much for him when a gopher scurried across his path and made him shout with alarm.

Deven steadied his tottering friend, while Brogg snickered.

"This is worse than I expected."

"Want to go back and forget about all this?"

Sten stiffened with resolve.

"No. This might lead to a government position.

Somebody has to start a new enlightened trend in governing."

"You're dreaming."

D e v e n conducted the newsman into the building and gave him a quick tour, equipping himself with a walkie-talkie so he could be in contact with the supervisors working across the site. Next they stood out on the concrete ledge that was used as an observation point a hundred feet above the excavations.

The site was a three mile long, one mile wide rectangle shaved out of the forest and aglow under the morning sun. One could visualize the day of devastation. The nuclear generator exploded and hurled a blast of superheated wind across the city, blowing apart the buildings. A monstrous fireball followed and roared over the cringing remains, melting everything and fusing debris to the seared and steaming ground while an awesome mushroom cloud billowed skyward and glowered with satisfaction over the destroyed city.

A few sturdier buildings remained partially intact, looking like stumps of scorched trees after a fierce firestorm, and only well insulated underground vaults survived undamaged.

"We blasted the rubble loose with nitroglycerin,"

Deven informed Sten, leading him down a ramp toward the excavations, "and then we piled it along the edges of the site." He pointed at the jagged mountains of scrap that looked like bronze sculptures of a nightmare.

"Why didn't you use something more powerful than nitroglycerin? That's practically obsolete."

"The government doesn't want me messing with anything more powerful. They're afraid I'll start a revolt or something."

"I see." Sten tapped the tip of his nose with his forefinger. "When did the catastrophe occur here?"

"In 2163. The same year as the plague outbreak." "No, one year before."

"Have it your way." Deven shrugged.

"How large was the population?"

"About twenty thousand people. Back then that was only a small city, today, of course, it'd be a major population center."

At the end of the ramp they took their seats in the back of a vehicle that resembled a golf cart.

"Most of the work here is already finished," Deven said, motioning the driver to start down the vitreous road that'd been crystallized by intense heat, "and right now we're concentrating on a mysterious pit at the south end of the city."

"Mysterious?"

"The thing's so damn deep. We've dug almost half a mile down and still haven't found what the clogged elevator shaft we're following leads to."

The glassy black road cut through a patchwork of square and rectangular rooms and foundations, many of whose interiors were undamaged and left in situ, all of the furnishings, including paintings, still in place.

"I compliment you on your fine work here," Sten said. "I was afraid I'd have to trudge through filthy trenches and root through heaps of garbage."

"Should've been here yesterday," Deven joked. "No, really I pride myself in my work. I've never been in a hurry to leave here so I was able to be detailed in my excavating, despite the city council's hounding me to hurry up. But I'm not in a rush for job re-assignment."

''You like it out here?"

"Fresh air gives a person a real sense of freedom." Deven stroked the scar over his eye. "Makes the city seem a prison."

"That's very dangerous talk," Sten warned, pulling his gaze in from the distance.

"I'd only say such a thing out here and to a friend

like you." Deven glanced up at a hawk that was swooping

low. "I only hope they don't have the birds fitted with

listening devices."

"Can you be sure it's a real bird up there?"

Deven gave a blank look, wondering, then was swept by

a macabre dream.

He was awakened by Brogg's call over the walkie-

talkie. "Director. We've uncovered an artificial surface

at the pit. This may be it!"

"On our way. "

Deven had the driver speed up.

"Could this be the vault you're looking for?" the

newsman asked.

"Yep."

Not far ahead was the rim of the crater where the

discovery was made. Mammoth earthmovers were parked

there and looked like grazing dinosaurs marshaled by

archaeologists. News of the find quickly spread and

a crowd of workers gathered like at the scene of a

fire.

Deven's vehicle pulled up to the pit where it was

met by Brogg who jumped inside. The cart plunged down

the rough dirt road and into the crater, bucking

wildly over the tread marks left by the earthmovers.

The moist clay wall funneled into an oval shaped bottom that was about the size of a baseball infield. A grater was still busy grunting and groaning as it scraped soil away from the widening concrete surface.

The cart skidded to a stop at the bottom of the crater and Deven jumped out first, almost banging into Brogg in his rush. He knelt on the artificial floor and pressed his palms to it. "Wonder how thick this is. We could try digging out the whole damn thing, whatever it is, but ... "

Deven snapped up, telling Brogg, "Send for a driller and an exploration suit. We'll see what's down there now!"

Brogg relayed the order by walkie-talkie.

"Shouldn't the city council be notified?" Sten broke in.

"It probably already knows. That eavesdropping hawk probably squealed."

"But ..."

"The council will get a report when there's something definite to tell them. For all we know, this might be the floor of something rather than a roof to a buried vault."

A few minutes later, a driller appeared on the rim

of the crater, a taller dinosaur than the rest, a Tyrannosaurus
Rex. Growling, it lumbered down the roller coaster slope
and stopped in the middle of the pit, its idling engine a
monster's breathing.

Deven hurried to the box-shaped cab of the machine,
got the exploration suit from the operator, and then
instructed drilling to begin. The drill was suspended
in a fifty foot tower at the back of the machine and would
bore a hole large enough for a man to fit through.

The drill started to spin, struck the concrete, and
tossed chunks of stone and clouds of dust into the air.
Deven and the others retreated to a safe distance
and watched the monster do battle.

5

The six corporalites of the city council hunched around
the conference table like scowling baboons. At the
head was a lean man with a square face, perfectly aligned
teeth, and radiant white hair. Though he was seventy-two,
he was considered only middle-age in this society. His name
was Limach and he was absolute ruler, using the other
corporalites as advisors and chiefs of various departments.

"The archaeologists have discovered the vault,"
Limach announced with a voice that made an indelible
impression.

"And the contents? Are they ...?"

"The vault hasn't been opened yet. They're
still drilling."

"So, we still don't know if the project in 2160 was
ever completed," Tias, one of the two women on the
council, said. She was head of maintenance affairs.
Tias had shrewd green eyes, coppery hair that seemed
to glow at its shaggy edges, and full pouting lips.

"We are certain, however, that the vault was
actually constructed and was well beyond the planning
stage."

"I hope the project was never completed." blurted
Jarla, a pink-complexioned woman with owlish black eyes.
"No one should have access to such a deadly force for
mass murder."

"That's strange talk from head of internal security,"
noted Vexxis, chief of the military and a man with a
snake like face to match his slimy personality. He
was the most jealous of Limach's power and in the most
favorable position to one day steal it.

"Such a powerful force as this can too easily get

out of control and destroy even the side that's using it,"
Jarla contended.

"Ah, but that's the advantage of this weapon," Limach
replied, "it will be under our strict control at all
times. Now that the premature detonating beams have
made nuclear missiles obsolete, and conventional armies
don't have the power to conquer the world, we will have
the only weapon that can ensure total domination."

"Under our strict control?" Jarla screwed her
tiny mouth. "That's only theory. We don't know what
will really happen once we unleash this menace. Everything
we're doing is based on one short passage in a top
secret United States military weapons report issued
in 2161."

"Indeed, this one short passage has accurately led us
to this secret vault," Limach answered. "Why should we
doubt the rest of the information?"

"We cannot take the risk."

"Cannot!" Limach clenched his teeth, snarling.
"We will risk it! The world is ruled by force and I
intend to rule the world!" He slammed a fist on the slick
desk top. "Force! And I will use it."

"He's right," Vexxis said. "With the state of the
world these days, where every city is practically a

country in itself, it's the perfect time for one great power to take control. We can be that power!"

"I agree," spoke up Rond, head of counter-intelligence. "The world is ripe for the picking."

Limach scanned the others and they all melted back. Tias would hold off until later.

"Vexxis, I'm sending you to the excavations to make sure that this last stage of the project goes right. This Deven is an impulsive, strong-minded person and I can't take the chance on what his reaction might be when he finds what's in the vault. We've already allowed him more latitude in behavior than normal because of the efficient job he's done, but his work is just about over now."

The slender, slithery Vexxis arose and headed toward the xeleporter. "I'll keep you informed," he said.

"Take whatever measures you need to ensure completion of the project."

"I will, sir. Whatever measures I need."

With that, the meeting adjuorned for everyone except Limach and Tias. They transported to their apartment where the discussion continued.

"Sometimes I can't understand you, Li," Tias said, dropping into one of the plush chairs filled with a spongy substance that had the softness of shaving lather but didn't lose its shape. "Why this insane urge to conquer the world?"

Limach braced himself by the wall and sucked in a cool breeze from the air-freshening module that was invented specifically for his apartment. He turned an unusually soft face toward the woman, saying, "When I was growing up — it must've been in the tenth year of the maturation cycle — I decided I'd see what it was like to have natural sleep. So, I fixed my slumber receptacle with a gadget on the edge that made the light on the outside register CLOSED when it really wasn't. After the overseer left, I'd climb out and curl up in one of the sofas. One dream I had was of ruling the world. It was the only one that didn't scare me and from which I didn't wake terrified. I had the dream again and again and decided I liked the idea."

Tias brought her knees up to her chin. "So, what will you gain if you succeed in conquering the world?"

Limach smiled, yanking a specially flavored wafer from a wall dispenser. "What will I gain? Ten million more enemies. Everyone will then want to depose the emperor. We all have our destinies."

"What use is the world to anybody?" Tias sighed, linking her hands behind her head.

"It's the fight that makes it all worthwhile." Limach sat beside the woman and flicked on the news screen by remote control. He left the sound off, however, the only person in the city who could. "I had a bitter struggle to reach my position as head of the council and could've been found out and executed at any moment for the whole year that I plotted."

''Yes, I remember that. It was an elaborate scheme you and the head of the News Bureau worked out. Day by day you fed the people stories about the worsening situation between us and the city of Kalferon and had them believing that each day they were being allotted fewer and fewer food wafers because of rationing."

Limach laughed. "And finally came the climax when the people feared they were on the brink of starvation, even though nothing at all had been taken away. The army revolted and I jumped from the lowest rank on the council to the top by promising food for all and an end to hostilities with Kalferon. To this day I'm amazed that the head of the council had been so blind. The fool actually trusted me, another member of the council."

"Oh? And don't you trust me?" Tias turned her face sideways to him.

"Let•s say I distrust you less than the others. Why do you think I made you head of the maintenance division? It's the safest place for you; one where you'll have the least opportunity to betray me. Doesn't that show you how special I think you are? After all, we've lived together for the better part of three years."

"Did it ever occur to you that I might not be interested in plotting to gain a higher position? Everyone isn't a deceitful, scheming bloodsucker, you know."

"Not everyone. Just most of the members of the city council."

"Why don't you just disband the council, then?" Tias waved her hand.

"That would be the worst thing I could do. I want my enemies where I can see them and calculate their moves."

Tias shook her head and thrust out her lips. She'd had many such conversations with Limach before.

"Twenty-two years I've been in power now," the head corporalite said. "And not much trouble from anyone in the last five years. Maybe that's why I'm so eager to conquer the world. A challenge."

"You speak of it as someone else might talk of a simple stroll down the concourse."

"It will be that simple if the contents in the vault prove to be what I'm looking for. It will be just that simple."

6

The drill relentlessly bored into the concrete, chewing out chunks of rock and spitting them into the air amidst whorls of powdery smoke. Archaeologists sat like amphitheatre patrons along the sides of the crater. Casually passing clouds gazed down and smiled at the folly of humans, glad they were safe in the sky.

"I learned what life was like here by studying the remains of the site," Deven told Sten as he struggled into the exploration suit which was as tight as a skin diving outfit. "It was certainly a better time to live."

The newsman turned away, trying not to be infected by stories of the past.

"Romantic love existed back then. So did the family. Know what a family was? An individual unit consisting of a wife and husband — something like permanent roommates — who usually conceived and kept children in the same house. The family stuck together when things got bad, at least ideally speaking."

"What's this have to do with..."

"Back then, people chose the type of work they wanted to do, it wasn't assigned to them as if they were robots. Maybe they weren't all suited for what they wanted to do, but at least they could choose from alternatives."

"But?"

"Government was a lot different in 2163, of course. It wasn't made up of a bunch of shit-head corporalites but officials elected by the people. From ancient newspapers I found, it doesn't seem that the old time government was

much better than what we have now but at least the
people could cling to the illusion of a freely chosen
government."

Brogg smiled broadly at Deven's diatribe, enjoying
Sten's squirming.

"A funny thing is that back then, when written
material existed, authors used to write books, called
utopian novels, warning about the dangers of worlds
like ours — the dehumanizing of mankind, the elevation
of computers and robots to godlike status, and the
destruction of Nature. Did anybody listen? Did
anybody act?"

"Will you stop!" Sten stamped his foot like a
schoolgirl. "What's the purpose of this speech?"

"You're a newsman, aren't you? I've just given
you copy for my obituary just in case something goes
wrong down in the vault. I want to be remembered as a
22nd century man, not of this century."

A dream flooded Deven's mind.

"Now, what was I saying?"

"Nothing," Sten muttered.

The grinding of the drill stopped, and the sudden
silence was startling. The drill bit had broken through
the concrete and hung in the hollowness of the vault's

interior at the end of a shaft twenty-four feet long. When the drill was withdrawn, a frosty cloud of air spouted out after it.

The drill bit was quickly removed and replaced by a conical shaped basket in which a passenger could be lowered down the shaft.

Deven strode to the hole and was fitted out with the various scientific instruments he'd take into the vault, Brogg hanging them on the loops on the front of the suit as if dressing a knight for battle. Deven's armory consisted of: a depth measuring device, an atmosphere analyser, a specially designed thermometer, and an air pressure gauge, all constructed to give lighted digital and alphabetic readouts. Lastly, Brogg slapped a powerful flashlight into his gloved hand.

Just as Deven reached for the basket, a helicopter buzzed from the north and nosed down toward the crater as if sniffing toward a landing.

"Look at the insignia on its side," Sten said. The emblem of a raven devouring a snake was over the door. "That's a corporalite's private copter."

"Just what we need," Brogg moaned.

The aircraft settled at the bottom of the crater, stirring a cloud of white powder. Once the dust died down, the side door slid open and Vexxis slithered out of the copter, accompanied by an armed guard of ten soldiers who kept their sear-rifles in firing position.

"Getting kind of crowded down here, huh?" Deven commented.

The high official marched directly to the head archaeologist. "I'm Corporalite Vexxis. Limach has ordered me here as official observer."

"Do you need an armed guard to help you observe?"

"A necessary precaution." Vexxis bit his words. "All important officials must be protected from the lower elements."

"Yeah, I can understand why."

"You'd better curb your insolence or it will be done for you?"

Before Deven could respond, Sten broke in, informing Vexxis, "The drilling into the vault has just been completed and Deven is preparing to go down to explore it."

''Yes, I see." The corporalite eased off. "Very well. Proceed."

Deven spun from Vexxis and climbed into the basket suspended over the shaft.

"Any last words?" Brogg light-heartedly asked.

"Yeah, I hope I don't end up in the South Pole."

Deven yanked down his radio-equipped oxygen mask, signaled the operator of the driller, and the lowering began. It was a very tight fit inside the shaft with scarcely an inch of room on any side. The grainy concrete walls scratched the toes of Deven's boots as he banged from side to side into a blackness that was darker than any that existed in Ixxendra except for the shadows in the minds of the people.

"I've descended six feet and the temperature's already fallen to fifty-five degrees Fahrenheit." He read from his thermometer. "Maybe this thing does go to the South Pole."

"Bring me back a penguin," Brogg joked. Though Brogg was in charge of communications, Sten and Vexxis could also hear.

"I doubt any are down here. The atmosphere is eighty-four percent formaldehyde, eleven percent methane, three percent carbon dioxide, and the rest an unknown gas."

"No oxygen?"

"None."

"Sounds like a deep freeze:"

"Damn! Twelve feet down, and it's now zero degrees."

"Underline what I just said," Brogg remarked.

"I could almost swear the darkness is increasing along with the cold."

No reply.

"All right, I'm down eighteen feet. Slow down. I don't want to smash into anything when I reach the vault."

The basket jerked as descent was slowed.

"Now minus thirty-one degrees and twenty feet down. Four more feet to go ...three ...two...one..."

The basket halted, dangling in emptiness, dangling in utter blackness and frigid cold.

"It's plummeted to seventy-eight degrees below zero! Suit is giving adequate protection, but it's getting nippy."

Deven flicked on the flashlight which had a beam as powerful as a searchlight's, and the vault exploded in brightness, burning his eyes. He needed several minutes for them to adjust.

The vault below gradually assumed shape like a film negative developing. Blurs became images and images took form — a large, grand organ shaped computer console, rows of silver, block tables, and translucent walls behind which were scientific

instruments. And lying on the icy, metallic floor were ...

"Bodies!"

"What? Repeat that."

"Bodies. Stiffs. Looks like four of them wrapped

in something on the floor."

Silence .

"Lower me, lower me!"

The basket inched down under Deven's

direction.

until it touched the frozen floor. He fought from the

netting of ropes and slipped toward the group of bodies,

each of which was wearing a visored helmet and lying

inside what looked like an aluminum foil sleeping bag.

Kneeling beside one of the bodies, the knees of his suit

cracking from the cold, Deven scraped the frost from the

visor and uncovered the face of a young woman. Her eyes

were closed, with frost crystals on her lashes, and her

cheeks seemed rosy next to her brittle red locks that

curled like mist under her visor. It was a face from

the past, and Deven was moved by it.

"What's going on down there?"

"Examining one of the bodies. Appears to be

frozen in suspended animation, and done in a hurry, too.

Probably necessitated because of the disaster on the

surface. I can't tell if she's still alive. You better send to the city for an expert on cryonics, I don't want to take the chance of accidentally killing any of these people."

"Right. We'll take care of it."

Deven rose, his suit having stiffened. "Tell them to come with protective clothes designed for a frigid environment."

"Right. Vexxis is anxious for a description of the vault."

Deven scoured the chamber with the intense flashlight beam which bathed everything in brilliant white. "The vault is rectangular in shape, about forty yards long and twenty yards wide. The place is obviously a lab of some type. I count about a dozen block-shaped tables for experiments, but they're all empty. Looks like everything was put away inside of wall compartments which are visible through a huge glass like screen."

Deven stepped to the wall and peered in at the objects behind it; culture dishes, microscopes, and other delicate instruments. His reflection stared back at him from the glass and he was startled by a hideous vision from the past, a vision of a man in a gasmask during the Third World War. Evil! There was evil

all around him, more chilling than the frozen air because
it was born of intelligent minds for the purpose of mass
murder.

The terrifying word fell from his mouth,
"Pestilence."

"What? Repeat that."

Deven thought of the Jovian plague. Could this be
where it'd been manufactured? Did the culture dishes
behind the wall contain the frozen organisms of the
plague strain? Was that why the vault was so important
to the corporalites? If so, the vault would have to
be destroyed. But he'd have to be absolutely sure.
Luckily, everything was frozen so that it was harmless
and would give time for future investigation.

"Is anything wrong down there?"

"No, everything's all right. But I'm going to have to
come up because my mask's frosting over."

"All right. Let us know when you're ready to
be hoisted."

Deven trudged numbly to the basket, got in, and,
after a final look, gave the order to be lifted. He
was tugged upward and the lab vanished as if it'd been
only a scene in a dream. Perhaps it had. The face of the
young woman lying on the floor lingered in Deven's mind

like a dream image.

"What happened down there?" It was Vexxis speaking.

"Busy."

"What happened to you down there?"

"Where's Brogg?"

Deven didn't reply, flicking off the flashlight, closing his eyes, and feeling the draft rush around him during the ascent.

The basket popped out of the shaft and Deven's eyes were once again stung by sudden brightness. He helplessly swung above the hole like a fish in a weighing basket, but didn't see just how truly helpless he was until his eyes fully adjusted. Soldiers lined the rim of the crater and a squad of helicopters had landed in the pit.

Deven kicked free of the basket, crying out, "What the South Pole is going on here?"

"The entire archaeological site is now under military control."

"Why?"

"It is now a classified area. All non-military and unauthorized personnel are to be removed."

"Including Brogg and me?"

"Especially you two!"

"You piece if shit!" Deven clutched for Vexxis

but was caught by Sten and saved from instant execution.

"Your job here is finished," the corporalite said.
"You will be returned to the city for work re-assignment."

Deven was about to blow up again but was pulled
aside by Sten who said, "There's nothing you can do.
Stay calm and live longer."

"I don't need any amusement center slogans, if you
please."

"Guards. Escort this man and the other
archaeologists to the monotrain," Vexxis ordered.

Deven reluctantly went with them.

Vexxis was intoxicated with the sensation of
power. Not only did he have seventy-five percent of the
armed forces mobilized under him, but a perfect,
well-equipped base from which to work. When would be
a better time to execute a coup?

Still, there was always Limach to fear. And Limach
certainly knew the volatility of the circumstances as
well as Vexxis. Could this be a trap?

7

It'd been three very long days. Three days
imprisoned in the sterile, climate-controlled city where
each day was the same as the last with little to do but
play mindless amusements, watch the news screen, and
smother in monotony. The worst part for Deven was that he
never discovered the mystery of the vault. Having worked

so long and been so close only to be denied the final victory was agonizing, especially when there was little hope of ever learning what was so important about the vault.

"Five years I worked on that damn project!" he barked as he paced the room while Rayniss tried to watch the news screen around him. "Just when I find what I'm looking for! It's like being on the verge of an orgasm and having your partner get up and leave."

Nodding, Rayniss petted the cat in her lap.

"I know it has military importance. But what? Biological warfare? We already have the science for that."

"Why are you worrying about it?" Rayniss asked with annoyance. "The job's done with, it shouldn't even concern you anymore."

"Done with! Doesn't concern me! It concerns all of us. What if they've found a new way to destroy the world?"

"Somebody would've done it by now, if that vault is as old as you say."

"Maybe they've already tried," Deven said, thinking of the Jovian plague.

"Then they must've failed. We're still here, aren't we?"

"Some of us are."

"What's that mean?"

"It means who can really tell what happened to make
our society as cockeyed as it is."

"Cockeyed?"

"Balled up," he tried again.

"Balled up?"

"Confused: Backward! Rotten! Miserable! Take
your pick!"

"I don't see what's so terrible about our society,"
Rayniss chirped.

"Claus! This damn place is like a prison. There
isn't any freedom."

"Sure there is. We can go to any amusement center
we want any time we want, go anywhere in the city we
want, and make love to whoever we want."

"What about freedom of mind? Freedom to think
as one wants. Freedom to be a human being."

° "Now you're being ridiculous."

"Am I? What if I wanted to get out of this asylum
just to go out into the meadow for a long peaceful walk
and have whatever thoughts I'd like? Can I do it?
No! What if the job re-assignment they give me isn't
to my liking, can I turn it down? No."

"What's the difference?" Rayniss replied. "Why care about what work you do as long as you get credits for it?"

Deven stopped in front of the woman, bent over and stared into her eyes. "Are you happy in your work?"

"Happy? No. it's just a job, why should it make me happy?"

"Well, satisfied, then. Does it satisfy you?"

"No. Should it?"

"Yes, damn it! Yes! Doesn't anything you do make you feel that it's worthwhile, important, useful?"

Rayniss thought a moment, then answered, "Yes, when I win a lot of credits at the video game machine."

"You call that satisfaction?"

"Sure, when I win," she twinkled.

Deven threw up his hands. He then pointed to the cat, asking, "Do you believe that's a real animal?"

"What kind of ..."

"Just answer."

"It's as good as real."

"But it's not a one hundred percent, honest-to-Claus, living, breathing cat."

"No. So what?"

"Pretty soon, we'll all be like that cat. The government's going to decide that mechanical bodies are

better than what we have and we'll lose our
humanity forever."

Rayniss considered the idea. She'd never be able
to have a baby if she were a machine. "But the
government's not really planning that," she tentatively
said.

"How do you know?" Deven mysteriously replied,
heading toward the xeleporter. "What if the government
is?"

Having become claustrophobic in his small
apartment, Deven transported to the concourse for
relief. He walked back and forth among the four
mezzanines, intermittently followed by eavesdropping
dustpans, and finally ended up on one of the outdoor
catwalks, clutching the ten foot high restraining
fence like prison bars and gazing longingly at the
sun-warmed meadow. Deven pictured a grassy copse
in the woods by the excavations where he used to sit
by a clear water pool and watch warm mist rising
from the glassy surface. To be there again. To enjoy
the peace and solitude and listen to the running brook
and hear the wind sift through the pines!

How could he escape this prison of a city, this

citadel in the midst of a maelstrom? Even if he could climb the restraining fence without being stunned by a patrol robot he certainly wouldn't survive the long drop to the ground. The only surface level exit was at the commuter station and its protective screen was impenetrable.

A patrol robot approached. Deven tried to ignore it, adding contempt with his indifference. Loittering was prohibited on the concourses and catwalks because it might lead to unlawful thought formation, like the type Deven was experiencing.

The robot stopped to duly notify him of this and remind him, "You are scheduled to appear at the breeding center in one half hour."

"All right, you big hunk of junk, I'm going."

As Deven started away, he spotted the air-cleansing fleet beginning its daily rounds._ "I could fly to Chicago."

— The stampede of catwalk strollers began and Deven was swept up like just another member of the soulless herd. And Nature was once again subdued.

8

Deven entered the auditorium-sized waiting room
which was already filled with over a hundred men eagerly
anticipating doing their part in propagating the species.
After announcing his presence to the woman at the check-in
desk, he found an empty chair and gazed up at the
theatre-screen-sized news screen on the wall. He'd
arrived just in time to see the first of Sten's stories

about the archaeological site.

Deven twinged with homesickness as the camera panned the deserted ruins and the reporter narrated, "What you are viewing is an archaeological site just outside the city of Ixxendra, Wisconsin. Due to a most incredible discovery here, all work has been stopped and the archaeologists evacuated. Found to be infesting several subterranean vaults of this destroyed, 22nd century city was a horde of mutant humans who apparently had been spawned by radioactive fallout from the explosion of the nuclear power station that obliterated this one-time major telecommunications center."

The reporter stopped, let a dream rush through his head, then resumed, "The city council of Ixxendra has not taken any drastic measures yet until the dangers these mutants might present to the populous has been ascertained. Until then, life in Ixxendra is expected to go on as normal. We will keep close watch on this fast-developing situation." The introductory report concluded. Significantly for Sten, it was getting national coverage and would certainly enhance his chances for a promotion.

"I wonder if the story is true," a thin-faced, pimply teen-ager said, leaning over to Deven.

He shrugged.

"Wouldn't it be exciting if those creatures attacked our city?"

"Yes, and kill off half the idiot population." He wished the story was true.

Deven wondered if Brogg had seen the report. He and his former top assistant had met while walking on the concourse and made arrangements to meet outside the breeding center to discuss the closing of the site.

"Deven WY6, report to room eight," came the echoing call over the address system. "Deven WY6, report to room eight."

Rising, he walked the length of the auditorium as he'd done many times before, passing through the small door at the back. Deven entered a long corridor which had twenty rooms on each side, and went to number eight. The room was a cramped cubicle, painted cherry red, and equipped with a large, springy bed, and a video screen across from it on which XXXX-rated films were shown; and an old-fashioned sink hung with towels was in the corner.

"Disrobe and prepare for copulation," a sultry female voice instructed him over a speaker.

Deven removed his one piece suit, hung it on a wall peg, and slapped over to the bed, the tile floor feeling cold and sticky to his bare feet. He lay on his back and readied himself.

The woman with whom he was to mate slipped into the room. She was about twenty years old, had long, shiny blonde hair, an expressionless face, mammoth breasts, and was smothered in geranium-scented perfume. She was a typical breeding center inmate, carefully nurtured to develop exaggerated sexual characteristics.

Silently, the woman lay beside Deven. She'd already had intercourse twenty-six times this day and was scheduled for fourteen more appointments — she had to conceive!

The woman stared at the ceiling with translucent eyes and remained motionless while Deven worked over her, she oblivious to him, not even blinking, just staring. Her breathing remained steady and tranquil even when he injected into the woman her twenty-seventh baby of the day.

. .
.
. . . .

It was over within minutes. Exhaling, Deven got up and went toward the sink. His mate quietly departed, still not having given a sign of ever having noticed Deven's existence.

It was the same for every man during his periodic visit to the breeding center. There was something highly arousing about a completely indifferent female to men whose everyday sex was usually long and furious.

The women of the breeding center were never allowed to leave the premises until their five years of service had been filled, they then being sterilized and given new roles in society. The children they bore were property of the state and reared by it until adulthood.

Cleaned and dressed, Deven left to meet Brogg on the concourse.

"I never did like these government operated whore bins," Brogg contemptuously remarked, lips curled in disgust.

"We have to take the good with the bad," Deven joked.

"I don't see anything in our society that is good!" Brogg had completely lost his sense of humor.

Deven also noticed that he'd become much more unbalanced and hostile since returning to the city.

"Did you see the news story about our site?" Deven asked as an eavesdropping dustpan began to follow them.

"No. I'm sure I didn't miss anything though!"

Brogg squinted back at the dustpan with ferocity.

"You said you wanted to talk about the site. What'd you have in mind?"

"What'd I have in mind! Getting back out there where we belong."

"Even if we could, the place is crawling with soldiers. We'd be arrested in a minute."

"Not if we follow my plan. Once we get there we could go to the storage room at the headquarters building, get some explosives, and take over the place."

Deven was nonplussed. "Have you gone batty! It's dangerous to even talk about something like that" He nodded back at the dustpan.

"I'll fix that," Brogg growled then spun around and kicked the eavesdropping device across the floor, over the edge of the mezzanine, and onto the level below where it smashed to pieces.

An instant later they were rushed upon by a patrol robot. The gruesome device faced Brogg and said, "You have committed an illegal act of destruction. This cannot be permitted. You must follow me for punishment."

"Go to the South Pole!" Brogg spat, pushing past the machine. Deven could almost see the robot redden with rage.

Before Brogg had gone three steps he was felled by a stun blast from the robot, which could've used deadly force if the crime had been serious. Deven leapt to the fallen man to see if he was all right and he too was shot by a stun blast.

When Deven revived, he found himself slumped in an acrylic chair before an acrylic desk inside an acrylic office.

"Deven WY6, former head of the archaeological crew?" asked the woman behind the desk.

He blinked his eyes and straightened in his seat.

o

"I am Jarla, chief of internal security. You are here for routine questioning."

"Is that any different from regular questioning?"

"Oh yes, quite. If this were regular questioning your chair would be electrified."

Deven appreciated the wit in the dark-eyed woman's response.

"To get to the questioning — what was the purpose of your meeting with Brogg MB8?"

"Just to talk over old times."

"Shall I replay the recording made of your conversation?"

"Okay, you already know what we were talking about so why even ask?"

"Because I want to know your personal motives." That seemed very strange, a corporalite who wanted to hear the other side of the story. Was Jarla trying to trick him, or was she a human —amidst her robot like companions?

Deven replied, "I honestly don't know what Brogg wanted until we started to talk. "

"Then you don't share his desire to return to the site?"

"Yes, I'd like to return there. But I wasn't planning on going by his route."

"And by what route were you planning on going?"
o
I hadn't made any plans at all," Deven told her,

gazing into her hazy eyes to seek deceit in them but failing. Was she an expert actress?

"Still, you would like to return there and get to the room with those explosives and take over the site."

"Ah, that wasn't my idea, remember?"

"Yes, of course." Jarla spun in her chair to think something into her computer terminal. She then turned back to Deven, saying, "That's all I need from you. You're free to go."

"Brogg? What about him?"

"I said, you are free to go."

Confused, he got up, looked askance at the bewildering woman, then headed toward the door, not sure what to think.

Brogg's situation, however, was much more dire. He was taken to a sensory lab where he was placed on a gurney and rolled into position so that his head was between two sonic-beam-dishes.

"What's this one here for?"

"Thought transfusion. He's a severe case of maladapted personality."

The technician jerked a nod then sat at the console beside the patient. Regaining consciousness, Brogg rolled his eyes to the left, saw what was about to happen and tried to leap up. His body wouldn't respond, welded to the steel gurney through electromagnetic attraction.

The sonic waves were activated. Brogg's brain was stung by ultra-high-pitched sound, and his eyes closed. The frequency was turned up higher and higher, pulsing faster and faster, and the patient plunged into a profound, unnatural sleep. Dreams instantly crashed through his mind one after another like fierce waves, battering his subconscious with fantasies. He mentally struggled against them but was hopelessly deluged.

Some dreams were terrifying. Some were just bizarre. But it was their overwhelming force that was so tormenting, submerging Brogg into a world of madness from which he couldn't flee. He could neither awaken, nor close off his mind but only endure the enforced insanity which annihilated his former personality like a hydrogen bomb detonating in his psyche.

When the mental maelstrom was at its height, a new personality was culled from the swirling madness. Brogg was given a new mind, a mind created from the slogans that were constantly droned at the citizens of Ixxendra in every public place until they sounded like echoing voices of the gods. Each slogan was the kernel of a concept of reality and a perspective on normal living which would blossom into a flourishing new psyche at the end of Brogg's treatment.

"Succeeding is forgetting."

"Live tomorrow yesterday."

"Dream less and live longer."

"August has two moons."

Each had a special subliminal meaning that was assembled properly during thought transfusion.

9

"The team of negotiators dispatched by President Drape to settle the dispute between Ixxendra and Tarro has been unsuccessful. Talks were broken off this afternoon when the representatives from Tarro claimed the Ixxendrans weren't bargaining in good faith. It has also been learned that the Tarronians have added more substantial charges including energy theft and high level acts of espionage to those of copyright enfringement already listed. The possiblity for war has greatly increased, and for an outlook on what this would entail we now switch you to our reporter in the field."

"This should be interesting," Rayniss said, petting the fixed cat that was purring contentedly in her lap. Deven grunted, more concerned about his predicament and why he hadn't been given a job re-assignment yet after having been removed from the site almost a week before.

"I am standing in one of Tarro's three main armories," spoke the attractive lady reporter, "and as you can see the soldiers are preparing for battle. According to unofficial estimates of Tarronian military strength, the city has an infantry of 2,500, an air force of over a hundred assorted craft, a tank corps of twenty-eight vehicles and a number of mobile defensive megalon screens. If these figures are even approximately correct, and there is strong evidence to back them up, they would make Tarro's armed forces one of the top five in the country. In comparison, Ixxendra would rank about fortieth, a merely average force."

Deven shook his head. "They're playing it like a

high level act of espionage is like simple copyright infringement."

"The possibility for war has greatly increased, and for an outlook on what this would entail we now switch you to our reporter in the field."

Was Deven dreaming this?

. . . .
101001111010101

"Do you really think we could have a war?"

"Could be -- and not over something as trivial
as copyright infringement, either. Ha, the National News
Bureau is probably negotiating for the rights to it."

Another news item appeared. "Also concerning Ixxendra.
Here is a follow up to our earlier story about the mutants
found inhabiting a network of subterranean tunnels apparently
since the destruction of the city in 2163. When questioned how
it was possible that these semi-humans could've survived for so
long underground, the chief archaeologist -- a picture of whom
appears on the screen -- replied, 'They received a steady
supply of air from a series of ventilation shafts and as for
food they most likely devoured the stores of edibles that'd
been kept in underground lockers for the eventuality of nuclear
war."

"Chief archaeologist!" Deven leapt up screaming
at the picture of the strange man. "Who is that fraud!"

The report continued. "Despite the significant find,

further studies had to be postponed due to the hostile nature of the brutes, having already claimed the life of Brogg MB8, assistant to the chief archaeologist." A shot of a man's body was shown.

Deven rushed to the communicator that was on the desk in the wall niche and hurriedly punched the buttons that'd contact him with Brogg, if he was available.

"I hope they haven't killed him for the sake of realism," Deven said.

"You don't think they'd really ..."

A voice answered the communicator, but not Brogg's.

"Who is this?" Deven asked with alarm.

"Vald. Who are you?"

"What happened to the man who used to live there?"

"How would I know? What do you want?"

"Never mind." Deven disconnected Vald and then punched Sten's numbers.

He wouldn't have time. The xeleporter hummed and a couple of policemen appeared.

"Come along with us!"

"Where?"

One of the policemen stepped forward. "Are you going to come peacefully?"

That was an odd request; they usually didn't request

anything.

Deven blinked farewell to Rayniss and then followed the policemen into the xeleporter. The three men materialized in an empty room in which there was a large, curved video screen. Deven was placed before the screen, then left alone. Next an image of a number of corporalites appeared.

"We have a special assignment for you," Limach announced without introduction from head of the conference table. "Since it is a vitally important mission, you've been brought here so that it can be fully explained to you."

Deven nodded, swallowing a knot of apprehension.

"Of the people you found the vault at the site — one has survived. The knowledge that she contains in her mind is of extreme importance to us.

We cannot risk extracting it in the usual method because this may result in irreparable damage to her. Therefore, we have selected you to persuade her to voluntarily offer us this information.

"Why me?"

"Because your ..abnormal ...fascination with the past should make her more at ease with you than with anyone else, and this is important in winning her good will. Also, she has lost a substantial portion of her memory due to the cryonic process and we suspect that you will be able to assist her in regaining it through your vivid, though offensive, accounts of life in the past."

"Suppose she's also interested in the present?"

"You will satisfy her curiosity in your own uniquely cynical way — up to a point! She must not become hostile toward us or our society. By the same token, we don't want her to feel as if she is being brainwashed, which is another reason we've chosen you. Do you understand?"

"Yes." Deven was surprised and unnerved by Limach's directness concerning his aversion to their society.

"I hope you do understand. If you should become too vigorous in your indictments against us and cause her to hesitate or refuse to assist us you shall suffer severe agony before being executed."

"How can I refuse such a tempting offer?"

"Be quiet! We are aware of your emotional addiction to the young woman named Rayniss. By complying with us, you will be safeguarding her well being as well as your own."

"A little extortion, too, huh?"

"Yes, if it suits my purpose. The subject of your assignment will be delivered to you directly. You are to acquaint her with our society and make her comfortable in it so that she will be inclined to assist us once her memory is restored. Remember, you will be under constant audio surveillance."

The video screen became blank. Moments later, the young woman he was to be in charge of entered the room, without a guard.

Deven was overwhelmed when he saw her, a woman from another age, a better age. Her face was round, her eyes were green and ripe with a sensitivity unknown to this era, and the blush of red on her cheeks matched the color of her wispy hair which hung a little past her shoulders.

Their meeting was awkward, like two teen-agers thrown together at a dance.

"My name's Deven." He respectfully nodded.

"I'm Delneen." She smiled with an honesty he'd never before seen. "You know, this may sound strange, but you look familiar to me."

"Oh, not so strange," said Deven, leading her from

the room. "I was the one who first found you in the vault."

They headed toward a nearby xeleporter.

Back in the corporalite's chambers, Vexxis was very displeased. "I still think it's much too dangerous leaving those two together."

" I must take the risk," Limach said. "Her information can save us valuable months, maybe even a year of work in discovering how to program the contents of the vault. Remember, it took all of America's combined scientific genius to work on it before the plague came."

"Our normal methods would've worked on her."

"Are you sure, Vexxis?" Limach pounded the desk, his straight teeth bared. "What if in our hurry to draw out the information from her mind we destroyed her mind instead. Then what, Vexxis?"

"And what if this Deven perverts her thinking so that she refuses to give us the information?"

"Did you hear my warning to him, or were you dreaming! The man may be a belligerent non-conformist, but he's not a suicidal maniac."

"Let's hope not."

Jarla entered the discussion. "I'm going to have them both under constant surveillance. Even if Deven should try to implant his own dangerous thoughts in her mind, I can have my people intervene before too much damage is done. "

"I'd feel better if I could have some of my staff involved in this," Vexxis said, sneering at the woman.

"This is a job for internal security not the military."

"My responsibility is to defend the city against outside forces, and this woman is an outsider."

"Your responsibility stops at the boundaries of the city. And for good reason."

"Then am I to assume that if we're invaded I'm not to act if the enemy comes inside our walls."

"Your job," Jarla yelled, "is to keep them outside our walls!"

"I think Vexxis is right?" Rond, chief of counter-intelligence spoke up. "This Delneen is an outsider and should be more closely watched."

Limach leapt up, shouting, "All right! Enough of this bickering. Although this is primarily a matter for internal security it'd seem a good idea to let the military also have a hand in this."

Vexxis gave a snake's smile, and was joined by Rond.

"But internal security will be in full charge of the operation. Understand?"

The meeting ended, but the bitterness lingered.

Afterward, Limach and Tias remained alone in the conference room.

"I remember once reading something about wolf packs," Limach commented. "It seems we have one of our own in the city council."

"And are you the head wolf?" Tias lightly asked, running her fingers through her shaggy hair.

"No, just an interested bystander."

"As a fellow bystander, I can tell you that I don't trust that Vexxis in the least."

"Like I said before, I don't trust any of them, but Vexxis the least." He played on her words.

"Then why keep him head of our armed forces?"

"To keep him occupied," Limach replied with a wry smile. "While he's busy thinking of all the power at his immediate command he won't be busy thinking about who might be preparing to take that power from him. Anyway, even if he stole my entire infantry while at the site, I could rebuild an army twice the size from our available citizenry within hours."

"Another plot, eh? I'm getting sick of all these plots. Everybody's planning against everybody else."

"Maybe you've joined the game, too. Have a little

treachery of your own brewing in that devious mind of yours?"

Tias laughed. "I'm happy being in control of maintenance, making sure everything's running as it should. It doesn't seem anybody's interested in taking my position."

This time Limach laughed. "In the last two months I've discovered three plots against you and in **all** cases the plan was to make it seem to me that you'd betrayed me. All parties involved were executed, of course. Naturally, the only people able to engage in conspiracy are those at the top levels which makes them even easier to watch."

Tias stared deeply into Limach's iron eyes. "How do you know I wasn't plotting to betray you? Faith?"

"Faith? No. You talk in your sleep."

Tias had to wonder, though, if all the supposed plots Limach spoke of were genuine or but figments of his imagination. If they didn't exist, his paranoia was steadily worsening.

10

Deven and Delneen began by strolling down one of the concourses where most of the symbols and activities of society were displayed.

"I'm still not convinced those xeleporters are safe," the woman remarked, walking with an easy, confident style.

"You'll get used to them. They're safer than driving

in cars."

"Cars? Do you still use them?"

"No, they're pretty much obsolete. But since I used to be an archaeologist I'm more familiar with things from the past than most."

"Like me? I'm a thing from the past. Probably obsolete, too." There wasn't any self-pity or cynicism in her tone, just basic realism.

"I'd say we're the ones who're obsolete. We've built an emotionless society that's following a course of planned obsolesence. When the last free-thinker dies, humanity will be obsolete."

"That's quite a gloomy outlook."

"Yeah, guess I do sound a bit like a bump on a log." He'd gotten his expressions mixed, anxious to make Delneen feel at home.

She understood his intentions and kept her smile of amusement hidden.

"How much can you remember of the old world?" Deven asked.

"I can remember what it was like, but only in generalities. I remember how we were always on the edge of nuclear destruction, but can't recall who wanted to destroy who. I remember things like the city where I lived and that I owned a car, but can't picture the exact building or type of car. And I was a judo expert."

"Can you remember anything about your work — what you were doing in the vault?" He asked for himself rather than Limach.

"No, that ...that's very hazy." Delneen shook her head and dusted Deven with her long hair. "I remember going to school, a university, and studying ...studying ... " She stopped.

"School! Let me show you how people learn these days."

"Okay."
Deven led her to one of the education centers, had her peek through one of the circular windows, and explained what was taking place. They then resumed their walk.

"What do you think?" he questioned.

"I don't see how you can have much individuality here."

"Yeah, but at least we'd all be smart." He smiled. "We could all be geniuses if the government wouldn't set a limit on how much knowledge a person could absorb. Who could control a population of geniuses?"

"Yes, the first thing they'd do is try to blow up the world."

"That seems to be a favorite thought of yours.
Why?"

"Because in my day that was the prime goal of
government, to destroy the enemy at all costs even if it
meant destroying the whole world. Don't you have wars
now? Have I awaken into a utopia?"

"We still have wars, but only of the conventional
type. The pre-detonation beams have made nuclear war
obsolete."

"I'd say that you have very much to be thankful
for," Delneen said.

Deven was startled by the comment, expecting
just the opposite reaction from the woman from the past.

"Tell me, Deven, how do you visualize my world?"

Deven then gave a repeat performance of his
oration to Sten just before going down into the vault.
He then gave Delneen a brief, but incisive view of his
society.

And the woman surprised him again with her
response. "I guess it's only normal for people of one
age to look back at the past and think times were
better then. Yes, in a manner of speaking we had all
the freedoms you brought up, but they were mostly
illusions." Delneen's memory had been jogged by the

conversation and she began to remember more and more as they talked. "True, we could love and marry who we chose, but very rarely did the relationship last for long. And yes, we could pick our own occupations, but quite a few people either didn't have the intellect for what they wanted to do, or simply didn't get the chance, so they settled for something far less."

"What about raising families, though?" Deven tried to save some of his fading image of the past.

"We were free to have families. But most parents were so busy with their work, and they divorced so soon, that very seldom did the true family stay together for long."

"And freedom of thought?" He almost whimpered.

"Have you ever read any philosophies dealing with the subject?"

Deven nodded.

"I doubt that freedom of thought, or choice, has ever existed. "

"Now you're the one who sounds gloomy."

Delneen abruptly stopped, hearing a peculiar noise behind her. She looked over her shoulder, saw the strange machine snapping at her, then fearfully bolted away.

"Wait!" Deven called. "What's wrong?"

He sped after the woman and caught her by the wrist.

"That ...that thing tried to bite me." Delneen pointed at the mechanical dustpan that was following them.

"Oh, that." Deven softly smiled. "It's only a maintenance device."

"But what's it snapping for?" She held close to Deven, quivering, her self-possession quickly wearing down.

"It just wants us to throw it something."

"Throw it something?"

Deven took Delneen across the concourse to a vending machine by the wall, saying, "I don't normally feed those damn things, but this time ..." He pulled one of the knobs on the machine, which dispensed an assortment of refuse, and scraped up a handful of crumpled cellophane. He then tossed it into the dustpan's gaping mouth, explaining, "If you don't happen to have anything on you to throw it, these machines are provided. I prefer cellophane because to me it represents everything that's unnatural and superficial about our society and get a kick out of ramming it back down civilization's throat, so to speak."

Delneen was dumbfounded by the absurdity.

"It also doubles as a listening device," Deven added.

"I feel like an idiot," the woman said, puffing out her blushing cheeks, "running away from a dustpan."

"You couldn't have known." Deven took her soft hand, which she freely gave. "There are plenty of bizarre things you'll be seeing in our cellophane society."

"I'll be able to handle them...as long as you're there to explain them to me." Delneen warmly smiled.

"Haven't seen one of those my whole life."

"A smile?"

"Not just a smile. A smile that comes from the heart. There's no such thing in my world."

"Maybe I was wrong when I said you have much to be thankful for in your world." Delneen stopped. "But look!" She pointed toward a building that had an aluminum Christmas tree on each side of its arched doorway. "At least you still have Christmas here."

"Christmas? No. That's a church — the First Church of Santa Claus."

"Santa Claus! You mean you worship Santa Claus?"

"Some people do. Only the ones who are fooled, the

ones who don't realize it's a government created religion which is meant to be foolish. A genuine religion would be too much competition."

"I see. It seems absurd on the surface, but underneath..."

"Yes, it's what's underneath that counts." Delneen detoured to the mezzanine railing and gazed down at the lower levels. "Tell me about the day you found me in the vault. What was it like?"

"We'd been digging for that vault for almost five years so it was a pretty big day. I was the first one down into it and found you and three other people wrapped in protective covering and lying on the floor. Do you..." Deven stopped as a dream slipped by.

"Yes, do I?"

"Do you remember any of the others with you?

"Vaguely. Very vaguely. One was head of the project."

Did your work have anything to do with biological weapons?"

"Microbiology...and computers . Those things
keep coming up in my mind but I can't finish the idea."

She was straining very hard, and her face was
flushed.

"That's all right," Deven said, "it'll come."

"It's already been two hundred years."

"Don't worry. We have a much longer life span
these days, more than 150 years."

They turned from the rail and started on.

"That long? Amazing. What do you do to keep
occupied?" Delneen asked.

"Most people waste their time at one amusement
center or another. Come on, I'll show you some 24th
century entertainment."

Deven led the woman into the nearest video game
hall. They dodged the thrusting hips and leaping
reflections and found an available machine.

"Long life is tomorrow," came the voice over the
public address system.

"What's that supposed to mean?" Delneen asked.
"Doesn't seem to make any sense."

"I used to think that the slogans were just for

indoctrination.   I then decided that they were really only meant to be confusing because the words have no meaning."

"Most slogans don't. Not even in my time."

They started play at the video game and spent the next couple of hours flitting from machine to machine.

Afterward, when they were back on the concourse, Delneen commented, "Those games are kind of addicting, you know."

"They're supposed to be. I think they're another trick of the government."

Suddenly, Deven spotted someone walking in their direction whom he very much wanted to see. He hurried over to the man with the frizzy hair.

"Brogg! Great to see you! I was afraid that ..." The confused man gaped at him, his eyes no longer squinting as Brogg's had, but full and wide.

"What's wrong, Brogg?"

"My name is Vald, not Bragg."

"What's the matter with you? Sure you•re Bragg. I've known you for ..." Deven stopped. No, it wasn't Brogg anymore.

A patrol robot skimmed to the scene. "This is an illegal conversation," it pronounced. "It must be terminated at once."

Vald eagerly departed, leaving Deven standing open-mouthed. The patrol robot also quickly left, as if it'd been a bad dream.

"What in the world was that all about?" Delneen asked.

"That man used to be a good friend of mine."

"But,but he didn't even recognize you."

"No. He's no longer the same person. He's had a thought transfusion."

"A what!"
"It's something you'll unfortunately learn about later."
Deven then motioned her to follow, saying,
"Come on, I've got to go some place to clear my head of all this."

Minutes later, the two were fitting on silvery space suits and screwing on helmets for a stroll across the surface of the moon.

"This is incredible!" Delneen gulped as they stepped from the decompression chamber into the barren lunar beauty. Rounded topped mountains that looked like they'd been covered with tight canvas lay on the horizon, shallow craters were sunk into the silty soil, and multi-colored star arrangements glorified the deep black sky.

"You ever really been to the moon?" Deven asked.

"No.   I once had the chance but was pregnant at the time and wasn't allowed to fly."

Delneen and Deven were enjoying one of the many holographic worlds in Ixxendra. Contained within vast buildings of glass walls many feet deep, holographic worlds were realistic replicas of either alien landscapes or periods of earth's past which were re-created by laser images projected through the perfectly aligned transparent surfaces. The lunar world was so accurate a copy that it was devoid of atmosphere and even simulated the moon's one-sixth earth's gravity, with conversations carried over inter-helmet radios.

"Too bad we don't have any worlds depicting your era," Deven said. He then added, "Although we do have the real remains of your former city."

"Ruins. That'd sure be representative of my era all right."

From the moon, Deven took his guest to a more mundane location, a movie theatre with a wrap-around screen for 360 degree viewing. Inside the door, each patron was given a pair of special eyeglasses, strangely reminiscent of the 1950's 3D movie craze. But in this updated version, the glasses not only allowed the viewer to see the holographic effects but also, unknown to him or her, a subliminal indoctrination film playing under the regular movie. So, no matter how contrary to accepted standards the movie might be — and many of them were adapted from past literary works — the viewer was constantly being reinforced in governmentally prescribed practices.

After the movie, Delneen commented with delight, "My goodness, 'A Tale of Two Cities' I remember seeing that almost 2 centuries ago?" She then massaged her eyes, saying, "But those glasses really gave me a headache."

"Yeah, they always give me one, too." Smiling, Deven took her hand like young lovers and led her to a nearby xeleporter, telling her, "Anyway, you've seen enough of our dismal world for one day and I think I should get you back to your apartment."

Moments later, they were there. And Delneen had a question, walking over to the bed. "When I was first brought here," she said, "everything about the place was explained to me except, since you have a slumber receptacle for sleeping, what's the bed for?"

"Lovemaking, of course."

"Oh, so it's still popular, huh?"

"Yes, like a sport. Want me to show you what I mean?"

"No, thanks. That's one sport I still remember, like judo.

Grinning, Deven stepped down into the main living area, glad she'd declined his offer because it made her truly different from the other women of his age.

"If you need me for anything," Deven said, "just punch number 1671 on the communicator."

"I will." She nodded, suddenly afraid of being left alone.

Deven entered the xeleporter. "One thing before I go — don't undress in front of the news screen. You never know who's watching you."

"But what if ..."

Deven vanished.

11

Delneen's headache had worsened. She wondered if there was any Xylox around the apartment, but there weren't even any cabinets where it could've been kept.

A hot bath usually helped, but her place didn't have the familiar sensi-tub, but had a kellator instead. Delneen decided to try it; it couldn't hurt.

Remembering Deven's warning about not undressing before the news screen, she drew herself into a corner and slipped off her jumpsuit. She then sneaked inside the kellator and pressed the cleansing button. A warm, wet mist tingled between her toes then swirled up her legs, across her abdomen, and to her bloated breasts fondling them with a cottony touch.

Delneen sighed; it felt so soothing, and the scent of violets was so sweet. Her pores were opened by the massaging mist and the soil and perspiration were steamed away.

When she floated out of the kellator half an hour later her headache was gone and she felt relaxed. After fitting into one of the many skin-tight jumpsuits that'd been supplied, she stepped down into the living room, eager to more closely explore her accommodations.

Delneen circled the two air-filled chairs that faced the news screen and fixed her eyes on the four foot high translucent pole in the center of the floor. Deven hadn't explained its use to her because it was a device he didn't approve of.

The curious woman stopped by the pole and sent a fingertip toward it, touching it. The pole became opalescent and sent a slow vibration rippling through her, warming her entire body. She stepped back, blinking. The sensation had been pleasurable, like a mini-orgasm.

She grabbed it, wrapping the fingers of both hands around the pulsing shaft. The vibrations were more intense, and so were the waves of pleasure.

Moaning, she sank to her knees and hugged the pole, pressing her cheek against it. The news screen flashed above her but the broadcaster's voice was mere babbling. Scenes of buildings exploding, people hanging on meat hooks like beef in a slaughter house, and satellites crashing from space were but smeary images to Delneen as the bliss overwhelmed her like a narcotic.

She remained in rapturous oblivion until the pleasure pole automatically turned off and seemed to throw her back on her heels, panting.

Her mind gradually cleared, and when it did she climbed into one of the chairs and deflated. She felt empty, as if she'd exchanged her vitality for a period of emotionless pleasure. Delneen also felt cheated, used, and a little guilty.

On the news screen a horde of mutants was shown leaping amongst a group of mammoth earthmovers, attacking their metal skins with spears, clubs, and fists. It made Delneen think of prehistoric Man. How long ago had it been since he ripped the hides from rotting carcasses to use for clothes, conversed by grunts and howls, wondered what the moon was, and was just another foul smelling, slobbering animal? Civilization built the steps for him to climb from this. Was it only to eventually change him into something that more resembled a soulless machine than a being of feeling? Maybe civilization had a regressive side effect.

"God, I don't belong here," Delneen groaned. "I'm a human being, not a robot."

She sat up and slowly, carefully scanned her apartment again, looking for a very specific feminine item. None of the sterilized women needed what she, a normal 22nd century woman, needed for feminine hygiene, which separated her from them almost as if she were a third type of sex.

"And for a moment I thought this was a utopia!"

There was a buzzing from the communicator and Delneen went to answer it.

"This is Tias," came an unusually soft voice, "One

of the corporalites. I'm calling to see if there's anything you need."

Delneen combed her fingers through her long hair and laughed, "Yeah, a ladyfriend from the 22nd century to talk over old times with."

The silence on the other end told Delneen that her humor wasn't understood.

"That's all right," Delneen said. "No, there isn't anything I need."

"If you're lonely I could arrange to have a roommate of any of the sexes dispatched to your apartment."

"No, thanks for the offer though." After a moment of thought, she requested, "Could you please tell me how to shut off this news screen for awhile?"

"I'm afraid it can't be shut off."

"Wow, at least in my time we could change the channel or turn the annoyance off."

"Sorry. Anything else?"

"Yes, I have this really strong taste for an apple. I don't suppose you have any here, huh?"

"Why, uh, no. They're obsolete. Sorry."

"Thanks anyway. Guess I have everything I need, then."

Tias cut off communication since there was nothing

more she could do for Delneen.

The woman from the past headed back toward one of the chairs, mumbling, "Doesn't anybody ever say good-bye around here?" She then curled up in the comfortable seat and dozed off, unaware how rare it was for anyone in Ixxendra to have nocturnal dreams as she.

12

The chamber was so quiet that the absence of sound made a person's ears ring. It had to be that way. The walls were fitted with a weaving of special electromagnetic material that distorted radio waves so that electronic eavesdropping devices couldn't penetrate inside.

"I assume you know why I've brought you here,"

Vexxis said to Rond, chief of counter-intelligence.

The man with the round forehead, bulging eyes, and puffy pink face nodded.

"I intend to take control of Ixxendra and will need your help to do it. You're already in trouble with Limach because of your blunder with that double agent so you haven't anything to lose by assisting me."

"What do you want?" Rond's thick red lips always looked wet.

"All the information you can gather. Keep abreast of everything going on with the other corporalites, especially Tias and Jarla. Kron and Zincs will remain neutral in the event of a takeover, so they shouldn't be any trouble."

Rond fixed his pop eyes on the opposite wall, taking accurate mental notes with his photographic memory.

"Most important of all is to know the exact moment when Delneen agrees to help. Limach is an expert in the mind siphoning technique so I'll wait until he performs it on her, which I know he'll be forced to do eventually. Once the woman has been persuaded to help, I'll put my troops on alert so that I can take over the second that the last phase of the project is underway. Then I, not Limach, will conquer the world!"

"In short, you want me to act as your private intelligence force." Rond blinked his heavy lids.

"Yes, you have all the necessary equipment and personnel for the job."

"And if Limach gets suspicious?"

"We won't have time to worry about anything if he does."

Rond lowered his eyes in thought.

"Oh, and if I were you, I wouldn't get any ideas about leaking information about this to Limach. I'll have you under especially tight surveillance with orders for your immediate execution should you try to betray me."

"Why should I tell Limach your plan? After all, didn't you just remind me that I'm already in trouble with him?"

"Yes," Vexxis said, "but betraying a planned takeover would be a good way to get back in his good graces. However, you wouldn't survive long enough to enjoy it." He reiterated.

"Do we have any other accomplices?"

"Yes, the whole army." The corners of Vexxis's mouth curled into a snake grin. "But my soldiers won't know what they've really done until after it's over."

"They won't care one way or the other."

"Neither will anybody else," Vexxis hissed. "Power
has changed hands like this since the reorganization
of modern civilization and no one's known the difference."

13

Driven by anxiety, Rayniss lunged into Deven's arms when he arrived.

"Oh, you're safe! You're safe!" she cried. "I was so worried about you."

Deven was startled.

"Where've you been all this time?"

He told her.

Rayniss was instantly jealous, an emotion she'd never had before and didn't understand.

"What's she like — this woman from the past?"

"She's very different."

"Yes, certainly superior to any of us. Anyone from the glorious past would have to be. Wouldn't she?" Rayniss dropped into a sofa. "Here I was worried about all the terrible things that could've happened to you and you're out having a wonderful time with another woman."

Deven was dumbfounded. She sounded like an old-fashioned housewife. "Don't get your dander up," he advised, sitting beside her.

"My what ?"

The communicator buzzed. Deven loped toward it, hoping it was Delneen needing his vital assistance with a trivial matter. It wasn't.

"This is Limach," grated the rigid voice. "You did well today. She trusts you."

Deven felt hollow, guilty.

"Try to accelerate her reacquisition of memory tomorrow. It's imperative that she assist us with operations at the vault as soon as possible."

"I have an idea that might help."

"Yes?"

"Let me take her to the vault tomorrow. Seeing it again might shock her memory back."

"Yes, an excellent idea. Transport with her to the commuter station at nine tomorrow. I'll have special passes prepared for you."

"Right."

Communication ended.

Deven returned to his chair. Had it been only a week since he'd last been at the site? It'd be good to taste the fresh air again and feel the sun on his skin. And maybe, just maybe, he'd finally discover the secret of the vault.

"What am I supposed to do tomorrow!" Rayniss squealed. "There are plenty of amusements in the city. Why not visit a holographic world? You've always liked seeing Mars."

"Not alone."

"I have my orders, Rayniss. What can I do?"

"Why don't you just move in with that woman!"

Rayniss stormed toward the xeleporter. "I might as well get used to going out alone."

"And I wanted a woman with emotion," grumbled Deven.

His roommate vanished. Would she come back? A bittersweet emotion swept Deven, but he couldn't define it. Rayniss was now teaching him new sensations.

A familiar face appeared on the news screen.

"We wish to extend our congratulations to Sten MOS who has recently been promoted to head of the News Bureau. His latest story about the mutant humans infesting the archaeological site near our city, and which will be made into a ten part series by the National network, has earned him the acclaim of the Ixxendran city council for meritorious service."

Deven was glad for his friend, but had to fear, "What kind of reward will the council give me for my service."

14

It'd been a furious night of lovemaking. Rayniss
should've been floating in rapture, but wasn't.

Trall's arms around her weren't as warm and tender
as Deven's. His kisses had been as fierce, but they'd
lacked the intensity of affection she'd become accustomed
to.

"I knew that you'd eventually come looking for
me," Trall said, grinning with conceit. "I was surprised

it took so long, though. It's been weeks since we met
at the video game center when you had that idiot Deven
with you."

Rayniss had run into Trall again while he was
playing one of the video games at the amusement center,
and this time accepted his invitation.

It was the morning after. Rayniss and Trall stepped
out of the kellator, dressed, then munched their morning
wafers. Spotting something interesting on the desk in
the wall niche, Rayniss headed toward it, her eyes
shining with wonderment.

"Is this it?" she asked with awe as she picked up
the puck-sized silver disc.

"Yes," Trall replied with great pride.

Rayniss giggled, running her fingertips over the
smooth, shiny surface.

The tall man picked the disc out of her palm and,
with a sinister smirk, held it an inch from her throat.
Rayniss stiffened, her heart ramming her chest.

"I'd only have to press this to your vein for ten
seconds and you'd be dead," the deathman told her.

"Is ...that how you get rid of unwanted roommates?"
Her voice quivered as she attempted some wit.

Trall laughed, but not with humor. He removed the death disc from Rayniss's throat and flipped it onto the desk.

"I guess that means you approve of me." She weakly smiled.

Trall twisted around and slammed a kiss on her lips which almost took the breath out of her.

Rayniss pulled away. "It's getting late. I have to leave for work."

"Too bad. I was just getting warmed up again."

Rayniss skipped toward the xeleporter.

"I'll expect you later. Bring your things here to my place." His face then became very severe. "Don't let me down."

"All right. I'll be here."

She gave the xeleporter her destination and was whisked away with great relief.

At the same time, Delneen and Deven arrived at the commuter station. Neither had had much rest the night before, and neither had used the slumber receptacle. Delneen didn't trust it and Deven felt it'd be a fraud to use it alone. He sneaked intermittent sleep in a sofa, but was repeatedly awaken by dreams.

They spoke very little during their monotrain

trip to the site, and not only because they were under
close guard. The shock of her new world had disquieted
Delneen and *Deven* was too excited watching the scenery
rush past to say much.

At the trip's end when he stood on the platform
overlooking the site, Deven was overwhelmed by his
surroundings. He swallowed the fresh, invigorating
air, rubbed the tingly sunshine into his cold skin, and
savored the scents of the woods and the fields. It was
a mystical experience! Deven vowed he'd never again
become a prisoner of the city.

"So, this is what's left of my city," Delneen said,
waking him.

"Yeah, and I had to do a lot of blasting to find
this much."

"I wonder if anything's left of the place where I
used to *live*."

She started down the ramp. Deven watched her
rolling backside and felt what he once did for Rayniss.

"Think you can remember the spot?" he asked.

Delneen didn't answer but continued on.

The site was like a military camp filled with helicopters, and soldiers, and Delneen was ever conscious of the two guards pressing right behind.

Finally, Delneen stopped only a couple of city blocks from the vault.

"This is it." She stood at the edge of the foundation square, her red hair tossing in the wind and uncovering a forehead which Deven hadn't realized was so elegantly rounded.

"You sure?"

Delneen nodded, her eyes tearing and lips quivering. The guards watched impassively with rifles held across their chests.

"I used to look out of our 27th floor window with my five-year-old son, Keldan, and point ...point out to him where I worked." Tears stained her flushed cheeks.

Deven slid a hand around the woman's waist. She was trembling all over and Deven was touched by the purest form of emotional contact.

"I know it's hard," he said.

"How could you possibly know? In a society of feelingless aliens, how could you possibly know!"

Deven was startled by her reaction. The guards indifferently shifted from one foot to another.

"I'm sorry, Deven." Delneen squeezed his hand. "I shouldn't have snapped. Yes, it is hard — very hard!"

He softly smiled and led her away. They were soon at the rim of the crater which housed the vault where much had changed. The elevator into the lab had been rebuilt — its ground level floor contained within a small building — the road into the pit had been leveled and paved, and the bottom of the crater was encircled by a ground rail which discharged a protective screen of megalon currents that dissolved anything that touched it.

"Must've been some important project you were working on," Deven said as they walked down the road.

"Must've been."

They showed their passes to the guard at the megalon screen and were admitted. Another guard led them to the elevator. The small compartment plummeted.

As they descended, Delneen quietly remarked, "Reminds me of my last trip down to the lab. Seems ...seems only days ago."

The elevator stopped and the doors sprang apart. A blinding white light burst before them and they stepped into it, blinking and shielding their eyes.

"Hello, Deven. Glad to see you," came a familiar voice.

"Do you know what happened to Brogg?" Deven asked.

"Brogg? Let me see, yes, him. I assume he had a thought transfusion."

"Assume?"

"How else could he readjust to civilization?"

"What about me, then? Is that in store for me too?"

"You've already readjusted. If you hadn't you would've had a thought transfusion by now."

"Oh, I didn't know."

Sten had changed. He was a lot calmer and self-assured and not looking as far into the distance any more, either.

They caught up to Delneen who'd squeezed in between a couple of technicians and was staring at their work. Her eyes grew wider and wider as her memory returned. She pushed away from the table, but didn't say anything; however, her shocked expression told Deven that she'd suddenly remembered everything and that the memory was horrifying.

Delneen folded her arms across her chest and said, "My, it's so cold in here." She shivered, but only partly from the cold.

"Yes, we better get you back out in the sun." Deven

understood.

"So soon." Sten said.

"She just thawed out a couple days ago, you know. And it's still pretty cold down here."

"Yes, I didn't think of that."

Sten walked to the elevator with them but stayed behind when they got in. During the ride up, Delneen said, "Last night, I saw this report on the news about how some of the old cities that haven't been destroyed are being populated by lunatics. I hope that story's true, because I want to be one of those lunatics."

The elevator was probably bugged, so Deven tried to warn her of this. "You can't believe everything you hear," he remarked. "There's so much news flying about that EVEN THE WALLS HAVE EARS." He stressed the familiar saying.

"What?"

"You know the old adage about walls having ears." Deven winked.

"Oh, yes ...yes, I see."

Shortly they were back on the surface and leisurely strolling through the site, enjoying the breezes, the landscape, and the cloudless sky.

"We were only an afterthought." Delneen sighed.

"What do you mean?"

"The freezing of the vault. The real purpose was to protect the specimens and keep them in suspension until someone dug them out. We were just a secondary concern."

"I'm glad it was done."

"I'm not so sure I am." Delneen hung her head. "I wonder why it took over two hundred years for you to be dug up. Why didn't they dig up the vault right after the catastrophe?"

"Maybe radiation levels were too high."

"Even so, they could've used protective clothes while working," Deven said. "I bet what happened was that the Jovian plague swept the country before they had the time to dig you out."

"Strange coincidence. But what we were working on would make the Jovian plague look like a simple flu epidemic."

"I'd like to hear more about that in detail. Maybe you could write it down for me in my old office. There still should be some paper in my desk if they haven't cleared everything out. As you've probably noticed, paper has become obsolete along with most other useful things."

"Like apples," Delneen mused .

"Ever since being revived I've been dying for an apple."

"Come *on*, then," Deven said, leading his guest away from the
site and toward the surrounding woods.

"My, it's so beautiful here," she hummed, sniffing
the forest freshness.

"It'd be nicer if we didn't have those two goons following
us."

"Maybe they'll get lost." Delneen's smile was like breeze.
Deven stopped by one of the wild apple trees. "Still green," he
observed. "The fruit won't be ripe for another couplemonths."

"Wonder if you and I have a couple months." Now a frown
shaded her face.

They were suddenly startled by gunfire coming from the site.
The guards quickly hustled them back out of the forest just in
time to see a pair of low flying jets skim the site and then
vanish on the horizon. No bombs were dropped or hits made on
the jets, with the entire event seeming like
a rapid dream.

"I just've came from Tarro," Deven said.

"Then the war stories are true."

"Maybe. Still, they could've been ..." he stopped as
a real dream ran passed. " ...just an act put on by our military.

dream running passed.......

"Why do you do that?"

"What?"

"All of a sudden stop in mid sentence as if a machine that's been turned off then on again. I've noticed that before."

"I don't know." He shrugged. "Everybody does it."

"I don't."

"You're a stranger." Deven grinned.

He and Delneen were soon climbing up the ramp to the headquarters building, then went inside. The two guards followed them very closely and became uneasy when Deven took the woman into his former office.

"You fellas don't mind waiting outside, do you?" Deven was being patronizing.

"We have orders to keep you under observation."

"Okay, how about if I leave the door open, then?"

The soldiers nodded and posted themselves against the corridor wall, looking into the office.

After sitting at the long acrylic desk, Deven opened one of the drawers, found a pad of paper and a pencil and pushed them to Delneen.

As the woman wrote, she spoke about an unrelated matter so as to confuse anyone who was ·watching or listening, or both.

"Since you're so interested in our society," she said, "I thought you'd like this piece of poetry that I remember being very popular in 2163. You can tell a lot about a society by its poetry."

Delneen finished and pushed the pad back to Deven.

"Yes, this is very interesting indeed," he spoke as he read. "It certainly does say a lot about your world." The last line stunned him.

Deven nodded. "I very much agree with your comment, too."

Delneen's comment was simple -- IT MUST BE DESTROYED!

15

They attacked without warning, without mercy, without
any other purpose than to kill. Invading one's body,
they penetrated the veins and deposited a substance
that interacted with the blood to make a person melt from
the inside. There wasn't any vaccination against them;
the epidemic would never subside.

More than simple viruses, their complexity was greater

than anything Nature would itself permit. They were
programmed to attack selected enemies and destroy them
with the basest type of malice — indifference.

They rapidly and abundantly bred. With this came
accelerated evolution and with evolution greater intelligence
due to their man-made programming and at last a species
that escaped this initial programming developed. The
intelligent micro-organisms then undertook a campaign
of organized genocide with the entire human race as the
object of extermination.

Deven foresaw all this. He knew it could happen — would
happen if he didn't prevent it. A species of virus created
by humans would wipe out mankind and become the new
masters of the earth.

Why did Deven's thoughts then turn to his childhood?
He formed a mosaic of memories of his youth and studied the
design.

After a morning spent with his brain plugged into
the knowledge disseminating computer, he was taken to
the play room with the other children. Boys formed into
one circle, girls another; and they all played the
game called, IT'S GOOD TO BE THE SAME.

"Now pretend as hard as you can," the instructor
said, "that you are the person you're standing beside.

See as he does, hear as he does, feel as he does, and think as he does. It's good for us to all be the same."

This lesson in conformity would go on for two hours a day, six days a week, during the entire eighth year of the maturation cycle.

Sometime Deven and Sten would be beside each other. That's the only time either of them enjoyed the game because they did just the opposite of what they were told. Deven spent the time doing mathematics in his head — the subject Sten avoided — and Sten concentrated on social conditioning, which was the subject Deven neglected. Deven conspicuously screwed his face while figuring mathematical problems and Sten just as conspicuously moved his lips in silent repetition of the social codes. How close each felt to the other because of this conspiracy they shared against the instructor.

This was the only good memory Deven had of his childhood. Partly because he'd escaped the grip of conformity when his individuality should've been squeezed out of him; partly because he'd found another person with whom to relate.

Sten later became Deven's best opponent at electronic jousting, a sport where the rivals sat astride specially designed chairs that were propelled toward each other on a magnetic rail. Unlike Medieval jousting, the loser would be pricked by a light-ray lance rather than having his bones broken and flesh torn.

It was a tension-stirring sport that afterward brought relief through flowing conversation.

"Makes me think what old age will be like," Deven once said. "You ever wonder about that?"

"What's to wonder about? Government policy is to place the aged in gerontic confinement to be cared for during the last five years of allotted life ."

Old age was determined to begin at 152. A person was then supposedly given five comfortable years in which to die or be put to death.

"I hear that they take you off the slumber receptacles," Deven noted. "Then you slowly dream yourself to death."

"It's better than being killed by a deathman. At least old age protects you from that."

"Think so? I've never seen an old person, have you?"

"No," Sten said. "But I've never looked for any."

"Maybe there aren't any."

"Well, if they've all died out, they'll eventually be replaced by new ones. People are aging every day."

"Yeah, but none seem to get old."

Deven's thoughts left his youth and returned to the viruses the government was trying to create in the vault.

Fortunately, the technicians were missing the last vital piece of information that would complete the project.

The monotrain returned to Ixxendra and Delneen and Deven transported to their respective apartments.

Deven found Rayniss sitting in the middle of the floor with her arms wrapped around the pleasure pole and her face smeared with the dreamy gaze of vibration-induced ecstasy. He strolled over to her like a cat following a weaving path, and tapped the woman on the shoulder.

Rayniss blinked open her bleary eyes that didn't seem hers.

"Having fun?" Deven chuckled.

"When?"

Deven bemusedly shook his head and took his seat before the news screen. It'd take several minutes for Rayniss's mind to clear.

"Early this afternoon, the mutants occupying the archaeological site near Ixxendra, Wisconsin made a surprise attack on the news crew documenting the discovery," the man on the screen reported. "One of the daring cameramen shot footage of the attack, just barely escaping with his life."

The gory but entertaining film began to run. Aware of its phoniness, Deven laughed as the horned, green-skinned bug-eyed monsters swarmed upon the startled news crew and beat on them with styrofoam clubs and jabbed them with spears of corrugated cardboard.

Rayniss crept into the chair beside Deven and assumed a contrite posture with her shoulders drawn in and hands crossed in her lap.

"I've never seen you use that pole before," Deven remarked.

"Never had to before." Her voice was a fleeting whisper.

"Had a bad night, huh?" He didn't mean to be abusive, just to the point.

"I've had better. And you?"

"Slept in the sofa."

Deven gazed at Rayniss's profile as she stayed rigid, A tear dripped down her cheek and her flaring nostrils glistened from crying. Deven was shocked by the sight, a sight that would've elated him just a few days before.

"Now what do we do?" Rayniss asked, sniffling.

"What do you want to do?"

"Stay here with you."

"Suits me."

"What?" She didn't understand.

"Stay."

"What about her?" Rayniss drew away a tear on her fingertip.

"Delneen? I think my assignment with her is just about over." Limach would demand results soon and force the issue.

Deven got up and stood before Rayniss. "Have you ever cried before?"

She shook her head.

Her face was suddenly a fragile image, blurry and moist like a still wet watercolor portrait. She was more tempting and human than ever before, but Delneen was so much more so.

"Maybe we can make up what we lost last night," Rayniss suggested.

"Maybe."
Like a romantic love scene, Rayniss rose to Deven's outstretched hand and they drifted to bed. However, for Deven the romance had died, though he tried to revive it.

Later that night, an intruder stole into their apartment to complete the nightmare. His tall, lean figure was a silhouette in the darkened room and was closely watched by eyes behind the news screen.

The intruder had come for revenge. Never before had he been stood up by a woman. Trall intended to make

Rayniss pay.

The deathman crept up to the raised level where she was sleeping in the slumber receptacle with Deven, and he knelt beside the device, his face warped into a skeletal grin. Withdrawing the deadly disc from his pocket, he then pressed the button that opened the receptacle. Rayniss and Deven were lying in close embrace, her head nestled beneath his chin. Maddened by the sight, Trall lowered the disc toward her slender throat.

Just then, a couple of policemen appeared in the xeleporter.

"Stop!" one of them yelled at Trall, who froze. "These two are not to be harmed. Limach still may have use for them."

Trall ignored him, thinking the guns were only set to stun, and continued his deadly work, pressing the disc onto Rayniss's throat. Both policemen fired at him and he dropped forward, dead, still pressing down on the disc. It was several seconds later when the policemen dragged Trall off Rayniss and removed the disc from her throat. She might still be alive.

16

The scanning center had three circular tiers and each tier was filled with monitoring devices that were humming, clicking and beeping with frenetic noise of city-wide surveillance activity. In the center of the bottom level was a plastic dome beneath which was a replica of Ixxendra where the location of every patrol robot, policemen and mobile eavesdropping device was shown by a red light.

"I thought it'd be a good idea to give the new head of the News Bureau a look at how the city is kept under constant observation," Jarla said.

"I appreciate it very much," replied Sten, standing by the dome with the petite woman.

"Your position is vital to the stability of our government. It's important that you see first-hand the scope of our operation and how necessary it is to keep the people off guard and continually guessing about what's really happening here and in the world. Despite all the electronic equipment, it'd be difficult to put down a full-scale uprising if something should ever trigger one. The best weapon is confusion."

Sten wondered why Jarla was telling him things he already knew, tantamount to a speech on official doctrine. Was she speaking for someone else's benefit, someone listening in?

''Yes, confusion *is* an excellent weapon. But it can also backfire and cause panic."

"Then would you suggest a more, ENLIGHTENED, form of news reporting?" Jarla stressed enlightened.

"Anything can be improved," replied Sten, following the woman to one of the consoles.

"Including government?"

They sat at the console. Its silver top crammed with buttons and switches glared under the almost painfully bright flourescent light.

"I'm afraid I don't yet know enough about government to comment."

The owl-eyed woman secretly smiled — she knew his real feelings, but not his resolve.

Flicking a switch, Jarla activated a five inch TV screen that was among a bank of them atop the console. Sten stiffened when the picture appeared. It showed two policemen carrying Rayniss' limp body from her slumber receptacle to the xeleporter.

"What's happening?" He controlled his alarm.

"One of her jealous lovers tried to kill her. I don't know if he succeeded or not. Let's see where they take the victim."

Jarla flicked another switch, getting in contact with a xeleporter surveillance operator. "Trace the destination of xeleporter XCL998M," she instructed.

Sten suffered a couple anxious moments. Then the operator reported, "Passengers transported to lab 97J."

Jarla punched a series of buttons and the lab appeared on the monitor, showing Rayniss placed on a gurney and left unattended.

"Can't tell if she's dead or just unconscious," the woman said, turning off the screen. "I'll know more later."

"Her roommate, Deven, is a friend of mine," Sten said. Jarla grinned, one side of her tiny mouth drawn higher than the other. "I know. I know all about you — who your friends are, what your childhood was like, what you hope to accomplish ."

Embarrassed, Sten blurted, "Who watches you, then?"

She pointed to a dime-sized microphone on her wrap-around collar. "He all have someone listening to us. The more power we have, the closer we're watched. All except Limach, of course."

"Don't you sometimes say things you wouldn't want overheard?"

"Of course I do. We all do. If we arrested everyone who voiced opposition to the government we wouldn't have any population left. We only focus on hardcore troublemakers, people who try to promote unlawful views. They have to be closely watched not allowed to go too far. Don't you agree?"

"Certainly." He was unconvincing.

"What do you think about your friend Deven's attitude?"

"I think he's somewhat misguided, but certainly not a threat to the government. You've heard our conversations."

"Loyalty to a friend. A rare trait. How deep does it run, though? Would you help Deven out of trouble with the government?"

"Why ask me that?" Sten hedged. "I'm not in so powerful a position to help anyone out of trouble."

"I'm not too sure of that." Jarla winked, then turned toward the console. She typed a message on a keyboard which was transmitted to a private citizen's news screen:

> REPORT TO BREEDING CENTER ON
>
> THE FIFTEENTH OF NEXT MONTH
>
> AT TWELVE p.m. SEXUAL ACTIVITY
>
> PROHIBITED UNTIL THEN.

"So, that's how it's done."

"Yes, a simple procedure. Each news screen can be given individualized messages from here."

"Quite impressive," Sten said, scanning the complex.

"Don't ever hope to do a news story on it."

"No, of course not. Who would believe it?" He grinned. Jarla got up and walked toward the xeleporter, behind Sten.

"I hope you found this ENLIGHTENING," she said, once

again stressing that word.

"Indeed so," Sten replied, stepping into the transporting booth, desiring more than ever to become part of this powerful world of the corporalites.

"I'll be in touch with you from time to time," Jarla said.

Sten xeleported to his apartment. A few seconds later he was drawn to the news screen by a message forming there:

MEET ME TOMORROW AT TEN A.M. ON
CONCOURSE TL9. DO NOT SPEAK, UNTIL
YOU SEE ME.   JARLA.

The message quickly vanished. It obviously had something to do with a matter of intrigue. Would it be a trap, or a way for Sten to realize his dream for power for which he'd do nearly anything?

Also curious about this was Rond who'd tapped into the monitoring system. He wondered what Vexxis would think of this development.

17

The slumber receptacle shut off, the lid opened, and Deven revived. He sat up and was shocked to full alertness by Rayniss's absence.

She certainly hadn't left him; not after last night! Had she been abducted? By who? Maybe a deathman struck and removed the corpse like an undertaker. All these thoughts swirled through Deven's mind.

He stepped into the living room where he froze before the news screen, trying to think more clearly. There wasn't any police department for him to report a missing person to. However, he needed help from some kind of official agency. The scanning center would know Rayniss's whereabouts, but certainly wouldn't reveal them.

The News Bureau: At least it was a chance.

Deven lunged to the communicator and punched Sten's number, more stunned than worried.

"Yes?"
"This is Deven. Rayniss is missing. I was hoping you could..."

"I expected your call."

"You know where she is? What's happened to her?"

"She was taken to lab 97J last night," Sten offered. "Some kind of accident."

"Accident! She was asleep!"

"I don't know what happened for sure."

"Thanks!" Deven ended communication.

He hopped into the xeleporter and was swept to lab 97J. Springing into the shiny white room, he angrily charged a lab assistant who wore a green smock.

"I'm looking for someone! I was told she's here."

The man stepped back with alarm.

"Rayniss. Her name's Rayniss. She was brought here last night."

Frightened by him, the lab assistant retreated to the check-in desk where he pushed a button that summoned guards who usually restrained delirium cases.

Two burly men stomped toward Deven.

"I'm looking for ..."

His arms were pinned behind him by the guards while the lab assistant rushed off to get a good old-fashioned strait jacket.

"Let me go, you jerks!"

Sten appeared in the xeleporter. Stepping down, he flipped his identification out, telling the guards, "I'm head of the News Bureau. This man's a reporter of mine here covering a story."

Deven was released.

"Who's in charge here?" Sten asked.

"Doctor Tenna," said one of the guards. "I'll go get her."

Sten led Deven to the check-in desk, scolding him, "You've got to follow the proper procedure. I wish you'd use some self-control."

Deven held his anger.

Doctor Tenna arrived. She was a middle-aged woman of 112 with curly black hair and hard hazel eyes that gave everyone a close examination.

"We're inquiring after a young woman brought here last night," Sten said, showing his I.D. "Her name is Rayniss A M 4."

"What's the nature of your inquiry?"

"It's confidential."

"Sorry, but I cannot give out any information unless clearance is given by a member of the city council."

Sten winced. How he longed to be a corporalite.

"I need clearance, sir," the doctor repeated, then wiped away an annoying dream.

"Uh, yes, contact Corporalite Jarla at the scanning center."

She did and clearance was given.

Deven and Sten were conducted to a dimly lighted room filled with people lying on gurneys like in a morgue. Among them was Rayniss.

Deven stood over her, clasped her wrist, and became as cold as she. He hadn't expected her to be dead.

"It happened last night," the doctor said. "Deathman, I was told."

Deven couldn't speak, just shake his head.

"Thank you," Sten said to the doctor, "that's all we needed to know."

He helped Deven away from Rayniss and toward the xeleporter, a moan reaching for them from behind, but not heard.

Later, at Deven's apartment, Sten remarked, "Her name was slotted for execution. Must've been."

"Only a society of madmen would murder a young, healthy woman for the sake of population adjustment." He was incensed. The government had no right.

Sten agreed. It'd be the first practice he'd end if he had the power.

He headed toward the xeleporter, saying to Deven, "I better get back to the office. Sorry about all this."

"Yeah. Thanks for your help."

o

"It was learned today," announced the news broadcaster, "that a number of southern cities has sent representatives to Deltannia, Georgia to discuss escapees repopulating the old cities. The much debated plan of sending military forces to wipe out what may become a severe problem for all civilized cities is expected to receive more serious attention at the meeting. Recent attacks on Platara, Louisiana by former residents of that city will be the main argument for those seeking a military answer to the problem."

Deven was reminded of Delneen and felt guilty that he was thinking about her when he should've been grieving over Rayniss. She had been his roommate for almost three months.

Escaping from Ixxendra and destroying the vault was his goal now. he couldn't worry about Rayniss anymore and Delneen would have to be warned.

Deven shuffled to the communicator and punched her number. There wasn't any answer. He then xeleported to one of the concourses to kill some time before trying to contact her again. During the long walk, he refined his plan for escape, a plan calling for air flight.

At the same time, Sten was meeting with Jarla. They'd transported to a holographic world -- the planet Mars — and strolled across the pinkish landscape of wavy desert and jagged rocks. Lighter spacesuits than those worn on the moon were used here, but the same type of radio-equipped helmet was needed.

"We can talk freely now," Jarla said.

Sten wasn't so sure.

"It's all right," she assured him. "We can only be

overheard by someone eavesdropping into our radio conversation and I've taken care of that by placing scrambling devices inside each of our helmets."

Sten nodded, his head seeming to float inside the headgear.

"The vault at the archaeological site must be destroyed," Jarla stated. "The fate of mankind depends on this."

Sten was dumbfounded, eyes wide with shock, though hidden by shadow.

"They're creating monsters in that vault," the woman continued, "micro-organism-sized monsters. They can think and breed and after they're set loose by Limach to murder his enemies they'll get out of control. Every person on earth will be killed. That's what we must prevent!"

"Why are you taking the chance of telling this to me?"

"As I said before, I know everything about you, including your strong desire to become a corporalite. If what I have in mind succeeds, there'll be plenty of room for you on the new city council."

"And if it fails?"

"It doesn't matter. Execution by Limach would be

better than to be infected by the viruses they're creating in the vault."

"How do I know you're not trying to trap me into something?" Sten asked.

"Ha! If I wanted to get rid of you I wouldn't have to go through all this trouble. I'm a corporalite, remember?"

Sten looked into the woman's eyes which seemed hazy and distant through the helmet visors.

"All right," he said, "what's your plan?"

Jarla laid it out for him.

A quarter hour later, Sten was back from Mars and striding down the concourse where Deven had last been tracked by the scanning center, information relayed to him by Jarla.

He located his friend near the First Church of Santa Claus. "I've got to talk to you about something very urgent," he said to Deven, squeezing his right hand into a fist which contained one of the button-sized radio frequency scramblers that Jarla had given him.

"Go ahead."

Sten explained everything to him just as Jarla had to him, including the part about the radio wave scrambler he was usinq to block off eavesdroppers.

Deven's part of the scheme would begin that night between the hour of 20 and 20:15, when, "Jarla will turn off the energy screen over the commuter station's exit. You will be free to leave the city and go to the site where you'11 have access to the explosives you used in your work there. The rest is up to you."

"Me!" Deven cried. "Wait a minute. You and Jarla are both in powerful positions, why don't you go?"

"For two reasons. We're even more closely watched than you because of our positions and would be missed if we escaped, you wouldn't. Second, neither of us want to risk our lives "When it's possible that someone else will."

"Me! Ha, at least you're honest about it."

"Both of us will help you the best we can," Sten said. "There's already a top priority pass waiting for you at your apartment which you can use once you get to the site. The only one who could question its authority would be a corporalite."

"Damn, you really thought this out," Deven ran a fingertip across the scar over his eye.

"If this goes as planned, we all gain. You get your freedom and Jarla and I will get much higher positions."

"Sounds good to me," Deven said. "I just hope we can trust this Jarla. I met her once, you know."

"Don't worry, we can trust her. She gave us clearance to see Rayniss, didn't she?"

"Yeah, but there's one more thing. Delneen's got to be told about this and be given a chance to come with me."

"What! Listen, the fewer people involved the better."

"Okay, so without me there'll be one less, huh?"

"All right, let's transport to her place."

They took the xeleporter to Delneen's apartment but found it deserted. Both of the air-filled chairs had been upset, showing there'd been a struggle.

"Shit!" Deven booted one of the chairs which flew across the room into a wall.

"The police must've taken her for some reason," Sten observed.

"I've got to get her back."

"Listen to me! The only chance we have is complete surprise. If we do what you want, we'll lose that one chance."

Deven considered that.

"Delneen would understand," Sten told him. "She

knows how vital it is that the vault be destroyed. She'd insist that you take this one chance."

Sten was right. Deven didn't like it, but he nodded in agreement.

"Remember, between 20 and 20:15 tonight."
"Okay. But one more thing. Promise that you'll do everything you can for Delneen."

"I will."

The meeting ended. Deven still had misgivings, especially about Delneen's fate, but Sten's plan was less risky than his and destruction of the vault had to stand above personal feelings.

Deven decided on a place to hide until twenty P.M., and transported there after picking up the special pass at his apartment.

18

Rond contacted Vexxis, who was overseeing operations at the archaeological site.

"It's about Jarla," he said. "She's plotting something."

A waiting silence from Vexxis.

"I don't know for sure what she's up to. She had a meeting with Sten of the News Bureau but something interrupted the radio signals so I couldn't hear what was said. Then, a little while later, Sten met with Deven, a friend of his, and the same interruption of transmission occurred."

"Obviously the three of them are planning together."

"Should I intervene?"

Vexxis had a terrifying dream of Limach and didn't respond.

Rond repeated. "Should I intervene?"

"No. Not until you can verify that what they're doing would interfere with our plans. Their plot might just provide us with an excellent diversion."

"Very well. I'll maintain close surveillance of them and see if I can find some way to break through their signal disrupter."

"Do that. And keep me posted."

Communication ended.

1011000101100

19

Limach stared severely at the woman, gritting his teeth into a perfect sneer. "I know that your memory has returned and you remember how to program the organisms," he told Delneen. "Walls sometimes have eyes as well as ears, eyes with telescopic sight, too."

"You saw the message I gave Deven?"

"Of course. He might consider me an imbecile, but

that's where he's hung himself - I believe the expression is - an
you are to co-operate and complete the final stage of the
project for us."

"If I refuse?"

"The information will be extracted from your brain
with a procedure that may not leave you wholly sane
afterwards. Now that I know your memory is back I don't
have to worry about extracting jibberish or a blank tape,
as it were. But it would still be safer if you voluntarily
give us the information because we don't know what little
bits and pieces might be lost in mechanical extraction.
It'd be greatly to your benefit as well."

"You're only a few weeks from completing the project
on your own. I'm sure you know that."

"We don't have a few weeks."

"Why not?" Delneen asked.

"That's not your concern. You're only here to give
us the information we need."

"To help you destroy all life on the planet. No!"

"That's strange talk," Limach noted, "coming from
someone who'd freely worked on the same project in the
past."

"I didn't freely work on it, not at the end anyway. When I realized the full potential of the project I refused to continue but my son was taken from me and used as a hostage."

"Oh, I see." Limach spread a sour grin.

Turning to the guards, he ordered, "Take her to the sensory lab," and he was then startled by a hideous dream.

Seconds later, Delneen was lying frozen on a gurney with her head between two sonic beam dishes.

"She had a son," Limach told the technician who was operating the controls. "Bring him back to life for her."

"Yes, sir."

Delneen was cast into a profound sleep. Her mind was pricked by sonic waves and Limach had her dearest memory resurrected before her. She was then forced to endure an artificial nightmare which to her was as real as anything she'd ever experienced.

"Keldan!" she cried for her son who'd been stripped and hung from a steel bar.

The red-headed, ten-year-old struggled in his bonds and swayed back and forth, grotesquely twisting his legs, looking like a matchstick figure with each leg pointing in opposite directions. Limach stood beside him with an electron tipped torment rod.

"No! Let him go!" Delneen shrieked.

"It's a very effective torture," Limach said with a
sadistic grin. He touched the rod to the boy's
ankle, jolting him with searing pain and causing his
frail body to wildly jerk.

"Stop! You have no right!" the woman yelled.

"The security of our city gives me the right. The
completion of our project is the best defense against
attack."

"It's not a defensive weapon. It's a weapon of
terror."

Limach wouldn't argue. He rapped Keldan's knee with
the rod and the boy screamed as the electrical charge
twisted and tightened his muscles into bulging masses of
pain.

"You're a madman! You won't know how to use such
power."

"Your son can't stand much more of this," Limach
warned. "You better agree to co-operate soon."

He raised the rod to the boy's peach-like testicles
and shot a jolt through them that was so excruciating
it stunned Keldan unconscious. The boy hung limp as if
dead with his tongue hanging out and his testicles
smoking.

"One more should kill him," Limach casually said.

"I'll tell you."

Limach smiled and lowered the torment rod. He then directed Keldan to be taken down, cautioning Delneen, "He'll remain in our custody so that you don't change your mind."

Next, he summoned a group of scientists to transcribe Delneen's instructions, which she gave while still in a dream-state.

Limach then motioned the head of his personal guard to him.

"Yes, sir."

"We don't need the use of this Deven anymore so have him arrested and taken to lab 97J for immediate thought transfusion. Lighten his skin a little, too. He's too dark for our society."

"Yes, sir."

The guard then xeleported to the scanning center but upon seeking Deven's whereabouts was told, "We can't locate him."

"What! That's impossible."

"Apparently the microphone in his xeleporter went dead so that when he left we didn't get his destination instructions. He can be anywhere in the entire city."

"Then you'll have to make a sweep-scan for him."

"Do you know how long that will take?"

"Do it!"

And the search for Deven began.

20

The woman on the gurney was rolled into position between
the sonic dishes.

"This one's been scheduled for a thought transfusion,"
Doctor Tenna told the technician. "Limach's done with her.
We'll have to use a different technique, though, because
she hasn't been properly indoctrinated. It'll take
longer, but..."

"What about the one who was brought in last night, Rayniss AM4? I was told to be ready for her this afternoon but she never arrived."

"That's been cancelled. She died a little while ago. She only revived for a few minutes, just as those two from the News Bureau were leaving ...

It was 19:30 P.M., a half hour more for Deven to wait. He sat on the last bench in a row of metal pews. It was quiet and dark in the empty church with only an aluminum Christmas tree for light. He liked it here.

Even here, he couldn't stop worrying about Delneen. His mind burned and time and again he was tempted to leap up, fly from the church, and search for the woman. Each time he stifled the impulse, feeling like a coward. It didn't matter that he was unafraid and that inactivity required more courage; it did matter that Delneen might need his help and he wasn't doing a thing.

The star atop the Christmas tree flickered. Deven looked at the life-size statue of Santa Claus beside the tree and wondered if he should ask for a present, preferably a weapon. He then noticed the sharp, metal icicles that hung on the tree as ornaments, thinking one of them would make an excellent weapon. He took one.

It was 19:44 P.M.

In the scanning center the search for Deven was still going on and widening in scope. Informed of the situation, Limach ordered a city-wide alert, putting all patrol robots and policemen on the lookout for the fugitive, suspecting that Deven's goal would be the destruction of the vault if he escaped.

Limach soon had another major problem. The Tarronian army had begun its march on Ixxendra and the first air strike was imminent.

"Do you think we'll be able to complete the project in time to repel the attack?" he asked one of the technicians.

"It's difficult to judge. If we begin immediately we may be ready by morning."

"All right. Relay what you've recorded of the woman's instructions to the people working at the complex. Keep a round-the-clock staff on it."

"Yes, sir. "

It was 19:51 P.M.

Deven was feverish with anxiety, not over his own fate but Delneen's. What was happening to her? Was she just being questioned, or was she being tortured?

Finally, his instincts overpowered his good sense. Deven had to help her if he could.

He bolted from the bench and onto the concourse. His footsteps echoed down the deserted mezzanine, empty of people because they'd been warned to stay in their homes due to the war threat. Only policemen and patrol robots were about and there were dozens of them.

Deven was quickly spotted by one of the robots which skimmed toward him, firing lethal blasts and signaling the other security forces to converge.

Deven no longer had a choice; he had to abandon any search for Delneen and try to make it to the commuter station which was three levels below and almost directly beneath his feet. He leapt onto a nearby escalator, ducked the robot's shots, which seared the steel railings, and skipped down the moving stairs.

Reaching the bottom level, Deven dashed toward the commuter station as policemen stormed after him from all directions. He dodged crisscrossing searing-beams and hopped over the fiery smears they left on the floor. At last, he wheeled into the commuter station and sprinted toward the exit with his heart furiously pumping, lungs heaving, and mind soaring ahead of him.

But had the electronic screen been turned off? Was it twenty P.M. yet?

Suddenly, Sten and several policemen appeared in the commuter station's xeleporters. On Sten's order, the policemen fired at Deven and dropped him with mild stun blasts.

Deven quickly regained his senses, was helped to his feet and hustled to the waiting Sten.

"You piece of shit!" Deven lunged for him but was restrained by a leathery arm.

"I'm sorry, Deven, but it had to be this way."

"You're crazy! Why go through all this? For what?"

"For a new enlightened government. Sacrifices have to be made for that goal."

"If our plan would've succeeded ... " Deven tried.

"Your foolish plot had no chance of succeeding. I always preferred the safest way, and this is it. Limach will reward me for this and I will take the advantage of my new post to press for reforms."

"Yeah, go ahead and help Limach murder all of mankind with those organisms from the vault."

"That won't happen," Sten calmly said. "You're a seriously paranoid individual."

"I'm paranoid? Ha! Well, if you're going to build this

new enlightened government on this type of treachery I'm
glad I won't be here to see it."

"I'm not. I wish it could've been done
another way. But time was too short for another plan."

Sten motioned to the policemen and they dragged
Deven to a xeleporter. They then all transported to the
scanning center from where Limach was directing
operations.

21

Deven was taken before Limach.

"I stopped him, sir, just before he reached the commuter station exit," Sten proudly reported.

"The electronic screen would've stopped him anyway."

"No, sir. It'd been turned off so he could escape." Jarla watched with horror.

"The only person who could've done that," Limach said,

is the chief of internal security or someone under her orders."

"Yes, sir, it was Jarla. I uncovered her plot and set my own trap for her." Sten smiled.

"He's a damn liar!" Deven yelled. "He was in on the plan the whole way." Scratching his hand on the metal icicle in his pocket, he withdrew the security pass that Sten had given him. "Have a gander at this. I got it from Sten."

Limach took the plastic card, which was punched with holes that only a computer could read. "Well, Sten?" He bared his teeth. "Is this true?"

"No, sir. It's Jarla's pass."
Limach handed it to a computer operator for an identification check. "If you're lying, Sten, I'll have you burned alive."

Limach then had Jarla put under guard just in case. "That's all Sten knows how to do is lie!"

"As if you're any better!" Limach roared. "In fact, you're a traitor, the worst kind of scum. Deserting your city on the brink of war with Tarro!"

"And you're a lunatic who thinks he can rule the world by killing everyone off! You're perfect for the job. It takes vermin to lead other vermin!"

Deven was clouted on the jaw by a policeman.

The computer operator returned with the security pass. "It belongs to Jarla LD31."

"So, Sten's nothing but a liar," Limach grunted. He turned to Jarla, snarling, "I can't even pity so big a fool as you."

"I wouldn't expect any from you."

"I knew there'd been some kind of intrigue going on," Limach offered. "'My secret security force had been picking up strange, scrambled radio transmissions. Until now I'd been suspecting Vexxis."

Unfortnately, Jarla couldn't prove Sten's complicity because she'd destroyed all surveillance records of his plotting with Deven because they would've implicated her, too.

Limach faced the prisoners, smirking. "Since we're on the threshold of war, we need more soldiers. You'll both be given thought transfusions which will leave you with only enough mental capacity to take orders."

And so he commanded. Deven and Jarla were taken to the same lab where Delneen was undergoing thought modification, a process which had just begun.

Deven's mind was torn when he saw her lying there, a helpless victim from the past.

"I'd rather be executed than be made into a machine,"

Jarla confided as she walked beside Deven between their two guards.

"I'd rather escape."
They were shoved forward. "Come on, you two, your places on the cutting tables are waiting for you," one guard mockingly said.

"If you have anything in mind," Jarla whispered to Deven, "you better do it quick."

Deven did. Sneaking a hand into his pocket, he grabbed his weapon. When the guards pushed them forward again, he whipped out the sharp implement, spun around, and plunged it into his guard's temple from which blood squirted like juice from an overripe tomato. Jarla lunged at the other guard but was drilled through the stomach by a sear-blast from his gun. Ripping the weapon from the downed man's holster, Deven fired a charge right through the other guard's face, leaving him twitching on the floor.

He then twirled around, shouting to the shocked spectators, "I'll bump off anybody who tries anything."

Nobody did. They understood his intent, if not his language.

Deven then shot a blast at the console from which Delneen's operation was being controlled, burning the

the device into a molten mass.

Delneen blinked her eyes, clutching for consciousness. Deven rushed to her, swearing at the technician who'd been working over her, "If she's not the same person I knew two days ago, you bastard, I'm going to burn your Claus damn head off!"

"We didn't have time to make the change," the fool replied, annoyed that he'd been interrupted.

Delneen opened her eyes and sat up, holding her throbbing head. "What happened?"

"That you, Delneen?" Deven stared into her hazy eyes. She gave him a quizzical look. "Well, who'd you expect?" She tried a smile but it was subdued by her pounding head. "And here I am without any Xylox again."

"Come on." Deven helped her up. "We gotta get out of this nut house."

"I'm all for that!"

Deven whisked the other guard's pistol from the floor, flipped it to the wobbly woman, and led her to the xeleporter. They transported to the port of the air-cleansing copters, a dimly lit, circular chamber with a clear-domed ceiling coated with bluish-white moonlight. The five small copters sat neatly on their

landing pads, ready for flight; and there wasn't
anyone to intervene. Yet.

o

Watch the xeleporter," Deven instructed, "and
shoot anyone who appears in it."

Delneen crouched in firing position, fumbling the
heavy weapon in her grip.

Facing the steel door, Deven unleashed a prolonged
blast at it, welding it closed. He then sped to the
podium-like control panel that worked the dome, and
he opened the ceiling.

"Okay," he shouted. "Let's get aboard."
They rushed toward one of the craft but were thrown onto
their backs by a nearby explosion. It was followed by
another and another, and several cracks wiggled
up and down the walls.

"The Tarronians!" Deven yelled. "Bombing the
city!" They got up and staggered to the chosen
copter through the rocking building. Just then, four
policemen appeared in the xeleporter and began blasting
at the copter. While Deven fiddled with the controls,
trying to remember, Delneen knelt on the floor
exchanging fire with the police.

"Hurry, Deven !"

Deven found the ignition switch and threw it. The

blades started spinning and Delneen closed the door, ducking onto the floor against the splash of sear-blasts. Faster and faster the blades twirled, chopping the stiff air and shoving the police backward with a gust of artificial wind.

Deven tugged back the ascent stick so hard that he feared it'd break in half. The craft leapt upward with a whoosh and fought toward the narrowing space in the dome which was closing due to one of the policemen's handiwork.

"Deven!" Delneen clutched his arm. "It's closing too fast. The blades don't have room."

The kill-thirsty policemen gathered beneath the craft and poured their weapon fire at it. Several shots stung through the floor, barely missing Deven and Delneen.

Finally, the copter burst through the scant opening, sheering off the tip of one of its blades, and beat away into the twilight sky. But there wasn't time to relax. Wedge-shaped jets with stubby wings soared through the night, launching rockets and dropping bombs on Ixxendra while tortoise shell tanks battered its walls.

"I'll be damned!" Deven cried.

"What's wrong?"

"Those are our jets."

"Attacking Ixxendra?"

Deven didn't reply. One of the jets began pacing them.

"Identify yourself," came the command over their
radio.

"Deven WY6, and Delneen."

"Who the South Pole are ... "

The jet pilot was interrupted and a moment of static
scratched silence followed.

"Accompany me to the archaeological site," Deven
was ordered.

It would've been suicide to disobey, since the copter
had lost considerable maneuverability and speed due to the
nipped off blade tip, so he complied. The small craft was
met by a couple of heavy military copters and escorted
to the site where it made a landing near the headquarters
building.

"From the frying pan into the kettle of fish,"
Deven remarked.

"No, that's, 'into the fire.'" Delneen corrected.

"Either way, we're cooked."

Their copter was surrounded by soldiers and a brutish
looking sergeant with especially big ears and a gravelly
voice tore open one of the doors, growling, "Out you two!

And leave those sear-guns on the floor."

They did as told and were marched into the headquarters building where they were placed in what had been a storage room. There was only one door and no windows in the dim, silvery room that smelled of printer's ink.

"What happened to the army from Tarro?" Delneen asked, sitting in one of the two folding chairs in the room.

"Who knows? Maybe it was all make believe."

"But Limach said..."

"Limach's mad! He probably hallucinated the whole thing."

Their conversation was cut off as the sneering, snake-faced Vexxis strode into the room. "Managed to escape from Limach, huh? That's quite an exceptional feat."

Neither replied.

"I'm going to be in control of Ixxendra soon," Vexxis claimed, "and will need some imaginative people on my staff. I'm sure it took a lot of imagination to get away from Limach. Rond informed me that whatever your plot was, it worked as a diversion for me."

"I used more brute force than anything else," Deven said. "You've got all of that you need."

Vexxis dropped the pretense of friendly chitchat.

"I'm offering you both positions on the new city council. You can be minor gods."

"Sorry," Deven replied, "I never visualized myself as a shit-headed corporalite."

Vexxis clenched his fists. "If you do not join me you will be executed."

Deven's mind ran blank with a dream.

"Well!" Vexxis woke him.

"I'd rather die by sear-blast than be eaten away by viruses."

"So, that's it. You're worried about the project in the vault. Well, I'm sure that Delneen can show us how to take the proper safeguards."

"No I can't. There aren't any proper safeguards." Vexxis pressed his slender face up to hers.

"I don't need you anymore, you know," he said. "The information you gave on how to complete the project was already transmitted to the vault. It'll be finished by dawn."

"Delneen!" Deven cried. "You told them."

"They tricked me." She hung her head, hiding behind her long red locks.

"She will still be useful to us as overseer of the project," Vexxis said to Deven. "But your choice is as I said before."

"You've got my answer."

The corporalite snapped up as if he'd been slapped, then marched to the door and summoned a couple soldiers from the hall.

"Take him out and shoot him!"

Delneen reached for Deven but he was tugged away by the guards.

"Deven! I love you," she called out.

The door slammed as the prisoner was hustled away into the narrow corridor. Deven frantically sought for a method of escape. He was being taken through the back of the building and his eyes flitted from door to door, seeking the one that led to the room where the explosives were kept. If he could get in there, and if the explosives hadn't been removed. It'd be a long shot, but he'd have to try it.

Deven skidded his heels, forcing the soldiers to drag him, their shoulders almost rubbing the walls. The explosives room was two doors ahead on the left. His body burned and the adrenalin surged. It was hard for the guards to grasp his sweating wrists.

One more door.

He was there. Deven lunged to the left, yanking his arms free, and burst into the storage room. Nothing had

been removed. He rolled across the floor to the
refrigerated locker where the powerful explosive was
kept plainly marked -- DANGER NITROGLYCERIN. Deven
hoped the soldiers knew how devastating and easily
detonated the now obsolete chemical was.

At least one of them did, putting up his rifle and
holding back his comrade's, when he saw Deven touch
his finger to the button that automatically opened
the locker. Ten steel cases the size of mailboxes were
inside, and within each case were twenty test tubes of
nitroglycerin.

Deven removed one of the cases and balanced it
against his chest. He slowly crept forward with it,
warning, "Either of you two try to stop me and I'll blow
this whole damn building to the South Pole!"

The soldiers backed out into the hall then dashed
for the exit as others watched in wonder. Deven yelled
as loudly and plainly as he could so everyone would know
the danger. "This is nitroglycerin. The slightest jar
will set it off and I have enough here to blow up the
whole site." An exaggeration.

Vexxis exploded into the corridor, dragging Delneen
with him.

"If you don't put that gently on the floor," the

corporalite hissed, "I'm going to kill her!"

He fastened a choke hold around Delneen's neck and held her in front of him, her arms dangling to her thighs.

"Well!" Vexxis challenged. "She's choking to death."

Deven made a quick move to open the case, which threw Vexxis off guard. Then Delneen acted, using her judo on the tall man, grabbing his arm with one hand, his neck with the other, then flinging him over her shoulder as she dipped to the left. She then jumped over him and rushed to Deven's side.

As they carefully backed down the corridor, Deven plucked out one of the test tubes. Before slipping out the door, he hurled the vial of nitroglycerin down the length of the hall, blowing to smithereens half of the building. Once outside, he removed another test tube and heaved it into the dusky distance like a hand grenade, clearing away a pack of troops who were stationed nearby.

Moments later, Deven and Delneen were back in their copter with the woman cradling the case of explosives in her lap. The damaged craft was rough handling, but Deven steered it across the site and toward the vault, hoping the nitroglycerin would be powerful enough·to do the job.

22

The sky was suddenly filled with the flash of artillery and rocket fire as if a pyrotechnics display had been set off in the early night. Bombs detonated across the site in pillars of flame and sleek jet fighters sparred at high altitudes. The long-expected Tarronian attack had begun and the tiny air-cleansing copter was in the midst of it all.

Fighting his craft, Deven flew on a straight line toward the vault, battling the impulse to zigzag through the dropping megalon bombs, whistling missiles and streaking rays. No one was aiming directly at him, but his craft was caught in the crossfire which was just as dangerous, especially with a cargo of nitroglycerin.

"The vault's just ahead," Deven yelled over the thunder of war. "I'm going to hover over it for ONE SPLIT SECOND, that's when you dump out the load of nitro." That one split second would be the most hazardous of all.

Delneen nodded, positioned herself sideways to the door, and grasped the edges of the explosives case with trembling hands.

A couple of sear-rays stung through the cabin of the copter and Deven struggled with the vibrating control stick to keep a level course. Hit by the concussions of nearby detonations, the copter bobbed up and down like a bird floating on currents, but Deven kept the craft from rolling.

The crater which held the vault was fifty yards away.

"Ready?" Deven called.

Delneen nervously nodded and she gave him a quick glance that told of her love, just in case.

Twenty yards. Ten.

The copter crossed the rim of the crater and Deven felt every rifle barrel, tank turret, and artillery muzzle swing toward them. He hovered a little above the rim. Delneen opened the door and shoved out the nitroglycerin. The steel case impacted, and the vault exploded in ferocious cascades of fire and smoke like a volcano. And Deven was struck numb by a deadly dream.

"Deven!"

Delneen leapt across the seat and yanked back the ascent stick into Deven's ribs, stunning him awake. The craft shot upward, just barely escaping the barrage that converged on where it'd been.

Deven steered the copter on a southward heading and away from Ixxendra, hugging the treetops for cover. But he wouldn't get away that easily. A couple of Ixxendran military copters hurried skyward and raced after him, flicking on powerful searchlights and sweeping them across the treetops. One of the lights caught the small craft and illuminated the cabin.

"Hold on," Deven said. He counted to two, then swung the copter to the left.

The rocket that'd been fired on it slashed by its tail, missing it.

Deven now flew the zigzag pattern that he couldn't perform over the site. His craft flashed in and out of the wildly crisscrossing searchlights like a moth under a streetlamp. Several rockets tore past the copter but were seconds behind its last position. However, the more powerful military helicopters were catching up to it.

"We've got one last trick left," Deven said. "Good thing it's a good old cool Wisconsin night."

He then drew all the way back on the ascent stick and pulled out all the throttles on the engines.

"If this works, I should get a medal from somebody." Deven smiled.

"I'll give you something better than that."

"This isn't any time to break my concentration."

Higher and higher the small copter climbed, its damaged blade not hampering it.

"You're not planning on flying me to the moon, are you?" Delneen nervously quipped, starting to shiver from the rapidly falling temperature.

"That reminds me," Deven said, flicking a switch which dropped a pair of oxygen masks from overhead compartments, "we're going to need these. The pilots and passengers of these air-cleaners who can't stand the ammonia smell of the disinfectant use the oxygen masks during their flights."

The military helicopters were still hunting them, against Deven's hopes they'd give up.

"How high are we?" Delneen asked.

"Don't know. The highest reading is 10,000 feet which we passed some time ago. We can't go much higher, though, because of the air pressure."

"So, now what?"

"Do you know why these are called antisepticizers?" The woman shook her head.

Grinning, Deven pressed the button that released the atmosphere cleansing solution. It rained upon the pursuing helicopters and, at this height, froze on contact with their twirling blades. The military copters dove down to warmer air to defrost. While they did, their prey got away.

Deven and Delneen plunged into a darkness devoid of city lights, blinking transmitter towers, and any other illumination cast by civilization. It gave them a cold, uneasy feeling, but also a peaceful feeling.

"I never seen such a darkness before," Delneen whispered with awe. "I wonder what's really out there. Does Chicago or New York or any of the other old cities really still exist?"

"Can't say for sure. There's one thing I'm sure of.
We're not the only ones to have escaped cities like
Ixxendra. There'll be other people out there and where
there are people there is civilization."

"Funny. We've just escaped civilization and now
hope we find some kind of civilization out there." She
pointed into the night.

"There are all kinds of civilizations, good, bad, and
inbetween. We'll find one where we'll be free to be human
beings again," Deven said.

"And be free to hope and dream."

"Yes, and...dream."

passing by

END

dream again.